Penguin Books
A Time To Kill

Born in 1900, Geoffrey Household was educated at
Clifton and Magdalen College, Oxford, and, on going
down, spent four years as a banker in Rumania.
Irked by the sedentary dignity of it he set off for
Spain to sell bananas, and from there went on to the
United States just in time for the Depression. After
writing children's plays for radio in the States he
returned to England, but shortly afterwards began
to travel printers' inks in Europe and South America.
Meanwhile *Atlantic Monthly* encouraged him to start
writing professionally, on the strength of his short
stories. His first novel, *The Third Hour,* was published
in 1937 and was followed by a collection of short
stories. He was unable to profit by the success of
Rogue Male, published in 1939, since he had already
been dispatched to Rumania as an Intelligence Officer
by the time it came out. He remained in the Middle
East until 1945 and then had almost to begin again
as a writer. After two novels which were set in the
Middle East he published *A Rough Shoot* and
Watcher in the Shadows (both in Penguins), *Fellow
Passenger, Thing to Love, Olura, The Courtesy of
Death* and *Dance of the Dwarfs,* as well as short
stories and children's books.

Geoffrey Household, who is married and has three
children, lives in the country.

D1332834

Geoffrey Household

A Time to Kill

Penguin Books

Penguin Books Ltd, Harmondsworth,
Middlesex, England
Penguin Books Australia Ltd, Ringwood,
Victoria, Australia

First published by Michael Joseph 1952
Published in Penguin Books 1971
Copyright © Geoffrey Household, 1952

Made and printed in Great Britain by
C. Nicholls & Company Ltd
Set in Linotype Granjon

To every thing there is a season, and a time to every purpose under the heaven: a time to be born, and a time to die; a time to plant, and a time to pluck up that which is planted; a time to kill, and a time to heal.

Ecclesiastes, 3

Roland had telephoned me to look him up the next time I was in London and, when I answered that it wouldn't be for a month, had asked me casually, but insistently, if I couldn't drive up some time during the week-end and have lunch with him.

So there I was in his flat with a silent, Sunday London outside. I fear I was very smug with self-satisfaction, warmed by the strength of the pink gins before lunch and a pleasurable sense of being wanted by a man who didn't lightly give his confidence. That I was wanted a deal more elsewhere did not, then, impress me at all. When Cecily and the children showed themselves a little hurt that I should use a free Sunday to go to London, I remember pointing out – I hope not too pompously – that I was still on the Reserve, and that an order, however it was given, was an order.

'You'll never believe who has had the cheek to come and see me,' said Roland.

'Somebody I know?' I asked.

'I don't think you ever actually spoke, but you certainly knew each other. It was Pink.'

Pink wasn't a man against whom I bore any malice. True, he had fired a few shots in my general direction, but even in them there was a certain style. He wasn't a treacherous, slinking, brilliant pansy like his former boss, Colonel Hiart. He was just a disappointed, simple-minded romantic, who had made the country too hot to hold him.

'Where's he living?'

'Alone on a boat,' Roland said. 'And he thinks it safe enough – what Pink would call safe enough – to lie low in the Essex marshes. He has grown a beard and nobody knows that he's in England. I ought to hand him over to the police. They want him for attempted murder and illegal landing of aircraft. But they would have more trouble in getting a conviction than he's worth.'

Roland always talked of the police as if they were a body of incalculable experts whose opinions must be respected but could only be guessed. I've heard a general discuss a cabinet minister in much the same tone. He seemed on excellent terms with Scotland Yard, and an inspector of the Special Branch had treated him, in my presence, with a grim and humorous deference. That indeed was all I knew of Roland, except that he had financed Peter Sandorski's underground. The only time I ever asked him a direct question – whether he belonged to the Foreign Office or the War Office – he laughed and said he didn't know himself.

'I'll put you in the picture,' he went on. 'Sandorski had a most valuable week in Vienna, and on the strength of his report we were able to act. The new fascism is just as dead abroad as Heyne-Hassingham's People's Union in England.

'But if you don't let political lunatics have one toy to play with, they'll soon find another. Members of the People's Union and its allied parties abroad have split like this: chaps who were trying to escape from monotony have taken to religion or societies with comic hats and chaps who just wanted to be ordered about have drifted towards communism. That seems incredible to us, but there it is! You'll remember that ex-communists made some of Hitler's toughest Nazis; and today in Germany it's the ex-Nazi who makes the toughest communist.

8

'Now friend Pink is a Brer Rabbit – allus somewhar, whar he ain't got no bizness. He's been in bad company, and on one such occasion he heard a couple of drunk German fellow-travellers blabbing away, all full of German tears and hatred, when they thought they were alone. So he came to me. He's an old fashioned patriot, is Pink, and born a couple of hundred years after he should have been.

'How far what he heard is a genuine plan or a dream of a plan or just pot-house talk worked up by Pink's imagination, I don't know. But this is it – Plot with the deepest, darkest P for communist agents to go round this country spreading foot-and-mouth disease.'

I said it was just the sort of yarn that any stalwart of the People's Union would think up to frighten old ladies and get their subscriptions.

'And the old lady writes her cousin, the general,' Roland added, 'and he to me, and I have to send him a note of thanks which doesn't look like a printed form. Oh, I warned Pink that he must think up a better yarn than that one, and told him to get back on board quick, or I'd let the police know he was in London. I wish now that I had had a little more patience. You've seen this, I suppose?'

He passed me a newspaper cutting. It joyfully reported the preposterous story put out by East German communists that American aircraft had dropped Colorado beetles on their potato fields.

'They must have minds like Pink's,' I said.

'Pink? Not a bit! He's thrashing the air all the time. Whereas these people – well, the only sure thing is that they calculate every move to the last place of decimals. And not a fault in the arithmetic – except, thank God, that their axioms are all wrong!

'According to our experts, Roger, this beetle story can only mean that they themselves have committed, or intend to commit or might intend to commit some very similar crime. Then, if they are caught, they can say it was justifiable retaliation.

'Of course, experts are always too ingenious, and I'm utterly unconvinced. The game wouldn't be worth the candle, you see. It's true that Pink's story fits their policy of pin-pricks in sore spots. But they'd be caught, and they must know it. And when they were, the fury and contempt in the Western world would be out of all proportion to the nuisance value of the epidemic.'

'Well, that rules it out,' I said.

'It should, and it does,' he answered. 'And yet I wish I had heard of this Colorado beetle stunt before I turned Pink out of my office.'

Pink had put himself completely into Roland's power – proof, at any rate, that he had made himself believe his own story. He had told Roland both the false name that he was using and the name of his little cruiser. She was too small and unimportant to be registered anywhere; and so long as he kept to quiet anchorages and didn't visit yacht clubs, nobody was likely to bother him until the end of the summer.

There was a warrant out for him, however, and if he drew any attention to himself he was pretty sure to be picked up by the police. Roland couldn't and wouldn't guarantee him freedom from arrest, and was most unwilling to have any direct dealings with him. So he had conceived the unprincipled idea that Pink should communicate with him through me. Had I any objection?

'But why me?' I protested.

'Well, he was going round at once from Essex to Poole on the track of his precious plot,' Roland answered, 'and as he won't be far from you and knows your part of Dorset well, I thought it would be easy for him to hop on a bus or a bicycle and see you after dark if he had anything further to report.'

I didn't receive Roland's proposal with any enthusiasm. The last thing I wanted was that bandit Pink turning up in the middle of the night and upsetting Cecily. I suggested that Pink's feelings towards me could hardly be those of a friendly caller.

'Good lord, he's too much of a fighting man to resent defeat,' Roland insisted. 'And anyway, he must think you were always obeying my orders. Love me, love my dog!'

'Look here,' I said, the dog taking one last wriggle towards freedom, 'if this tale were true, Pink couldn't have got hold of it. I've no idea what his contacts have been, but I'll bet anything they are just nasty, international small fry, who wouldn't be trusted by a responsible communist any more than by you.'

'My dear Roger, you're perfectly right,' he replied. 'But life would be very simple if I only used people I could trust. And the same goes for them. So be a good fellow, and let me tell Pink that he can call on you if he must.'

Thinking it all over on my drive home, I came to the conclusion that Pink was unlikely to bother me. His whole story was an extravagant effort to put himself right with the police, and I was surprised that Roland even thought him worth an envelope and stamp. He was certainly giving him no more – no help, no money and no faith. Pink could be counted on to compromise any organization which used him.

I made good time – considering the road was full of Sunday evening traffic going in the opposite direction – and arrived home before Jerry's and George's bedtime. It was a glorious June evening; so, to give them a treat, Cecily and I pretended to make a picnic out of their simple supper, and drove them up to Hardy's Monument to eat it. We could see a hundred miles of the Channel, all the way from the Needles to Start Point.

The slim, grey streaks of the warships in Portland Harbour made me feel more kindly towards Pink. Somewhere he was in all that blue, alone in his boat, a white speck lost at five miles distance, without wife or children and looking back on his broken career as a sailor. But if he *would* think he was Nelson, what did he expect? You can't disobey orders and get away with it – at least, you can't if you're a bull-headed lunatic like Pink. And then, after that, to take up with the People's Union and run the risk of being tried for high treason! No, his thoughts while he cooked and lived and slept in his twelve-by-six cabin must have been dark as the mud beneath his keel.

The children were dashing about, picking up spent cartridges from the heather, when Cecily asked me how the interview with Roland had gone. I said that he wanted to use me as a post-box – which, so far as it went, was true. There was no point in worrying her with Pink's morbid inventions.

'Is that all?' she asked.

'It's all he's going to get,' I answered positively.

I meant it, too, as I watched my boys tumbling after each other in and out of the hollows, their faces glowing in the last rays of the red sun. Then Cecily began to fuss because they hadn't enough sweaters on; so we chased and caught them, and took them home to bed.

I gave little more thought to Pink and Roland, except to wish in moments of disgruntled self-analysis – the ten minutes, for example, while one shaves a solemn and far too familiar face – that I hadn't gone rushing off to London so easily. I knew very well that my motive had been sheer vanity, for I needed nothing, and least of all Roland's complications, to put more interest into my life.

After all the excitement on my bit of rough shooting, I was for a few months a minor celebrity in South Dorset. Everyone knew that I had been wanted for murder – though only for a single night – and that I had come out of it all with a mysterious and official pat on the back. So, of course, it was generally decided that I was Something in the Secret Service, and Mr and Mrs Roger Taine began to receive a crop of un-wanted invitations from people who felt it their duty to know what had happened, and whether there was any con-nexion between the aircraft which had landed on the Downs, and the suicide of Heyne-Hassingham. I told them to ask the local police (who knew very little, but certainly weren't going to admit it) and my value as a county curiosity soon fell off. It was good for business, however. I got a lot of new clients among the builders and builders' merchants who merely wanted to have a look at me, and I managed to keep most of them – thanks to the first-class stuff our group pro-duces, for I'm never any good at talking a man into ordering what he doesn't want. So all was well at home, and trade so steady that I actually managed to save a little capital from the income tax collector. I was a contented man, and knew it.

About three weeks after my lunch with Roland, Pink called me up at the office. He was discreet, though hearty, and I couldn't make out who he was until he said that I owed him a motor cycle. I apologized for smashing it, and assured him, feeling a tactless barbarian, that I had hoped it belonged to the Party. No, he replied, his; but it really didn't matter. That we could have so polite a conversation amazed me; yet I ought to have known that Pink's manners – how-ever detestable his character – would come out of the top drawer.

He asked me to drive over and see him. I was to leave my car at a point near Lytchett Minster, and meet him at the head of an obscure creek where he would pick me up with the pram, and take me on board his boat. I must have hesi-tated, for he said in rather the tone of a sulky schoolboy:

'Look here – give you my word of honour!'

It was a grey afternoon, with the chill north wind of a beastly summer day, when I followed the cart-track down to his creek. Poole Harbour was at its most melancholy. It is a queer place of moods, with the four tides and the still mud-banks, bald or rush-grown, that disappear, imperceptibly, under the sea. It can be a gay, closed, little yachtsman's paradise of blue and white, or a sunlit lake among golden heath, or, as it was that afternoon, a dull, endless marsh that made me conscious of the mud at the bottom and the reeds waving up from it like dead men's hair.

Pink was at the rendezvous, standing in his sea-boots as still as a heron. Our earlier meetings, in dusk or at night, had never really shown him to me. He was an uncompromising figure in his shabby blue jersey, slim at the hips and broad as a fallen angel across his shoulders. His nose was slightly twisted to one side and his forehead was scored with deep puzzled wrinkles. The brown beard gave him distinction. Without that, I might have found his face a shade brutal.

He held out his hand as if we had just met in Piccadilly after long absence. I would have shaken it more warmly if he had not been quite so casual.

'I wouldn't have known you,' he said. 'I thought you were a smaller man.'

'The light, no doubt,' I answered.

'Yes,' he said, 'yes –' and gave a short, despairing choke of dry laughter. 'Well, come along!'

I sat cautiously in the stern of his eight-foot pram, while he filled all the rest of it and paddled us down the creek. His boat, *Olwen*, lay at anchor in a brown pool which the scour of the tide had bitten out of the flank of a reed-covered island. There were two narrow channels on either side of the island up which the flood was making, and would have to make for another hour before *Olwen* could twist a snipe's course out into the harbour. She could only be seen from the farmlands to the north. The anchorage was even lonelier than any I had imagined for Pink.

She was a thirty-foot boat with a turtle deck forward, an open cockpit, and no virtues to my landsman's eye except that she was obviously meant to be used in all weathers. When we were on board, I could see that she drew a foot or two more water than I had thought. There was good head-room in the single cabin.

I had expected to find the disorder of a lonely and demoral-ized man; but I had forgotten Pink's naval training. *Olwen* was packed so tight with stores and gear that one seemed to be standing in the middle of an expensively fitted dressing-case. The lids and doors of innumerable lockers were all closed and all neatly painted. There was a fairly clean, dark-blue cover on the settee, and very clean curtains framing the ports. Two shelves of books – mostly nautical almanacs and such-like – had been built around the shining brass chrono-meter. Drinks were laid out ready, the bottles reflected in the teak of the little cabin table.

Pink was very cordial. I might have been visiting any well-bred eccentric who chose to live alone on a boat. I hated to refer to business (which had inevitably to involve some refer-ence to the past), but Roland would certainly want, besides whatever message for him Pink might have, some kind of report from me on the man.

'You've lived on board ever since . . .?' I began.

'No. Portugal at first – till it got too hot. Some of the leaders of our Movement began to play around with com-munists. You know all about that.'

I didn't. But there was no point in disillusioning him if he chose to think that I was and always had been in Roland's confidence.

'You got tarred with the same brush?' I asked.

'Yes. God, what a lot of scum! They approached me directly. They knew all about my past and had the impudence to sympathize. Said they wanted chaps of my sort. The leader class.'

His beastly fascist phrase nearly drew a protest from me, but I turned it into a grunt of understanding.

'They do,' he went on, 'badly. But they won't keep 'em alive a day longer than they can use 'em. Well, I did some jobs for them. I thought I might find out a thing or two. That was the only reason. I expect you to believe it,' he added, looking me hard in the eyes.

I had no difficulty in believing it. If there ever was a dyed-in-the-wool anti-communist, it was Pink.

'Didn't they suspect you?' I asked.

'Less than you'd think. They can't understand a man being a patriot when he's been as badly treated as I have. And then – I don't know whether Roland told you – they framed me. One of the jobs I did – well, no need to go into details, but it was an extraditable crime. Anywhere. They took the trouble to show me the evidence they would use if I ever turned nasty.'

That seemed a powerful proof of Pink's good faith – if it were true.

'They know what you have found out?'

'Impossible. It was a pure accident, my overhearing those chaps. And no one saw me enter or leave.'

'And where you are – I suppose they know that?'

'I can't be sure, but it's unlikely. I bought this old lady' – he patted the white-painted curve that separated us from the sea – 'for cash, and filled her up with fuel and made England in one hop. Then I began to follow up the tip I had got. I'm ready now. I'm going to use my own methods. And you're just the man I'd like to have with me.'

I thanked him for his good opinion – there was no point

in telling him that his own methods were certain to be disastrous – and said I was there to help him.

'Then you'll come with me,' he ordered – I swear it was an order – 'to burgle a house in Bournemouth.'

'Sorry!' I said. 'No!'

'A communist's house. You can't refuse.'

'But how the hell am I to know it's a communist's house? And even if it was!'

My broad grin spoilt his fantasy. He saw himself for the moment, I think, as a gallant, outlaw captain whose commands could only meet with instant acceptance or cowardly refusal. It was a shock to him that I should find those commands merely comic.

'I forgot,' he said. 'Damn it, why should any of you trust me?'

I explained apologetically that it was just the idea of Bournemouth communists which I couldn't take seriously.

'Why not?' he asked.

'Oh, it's so blasted full of gentility.'

'Wherever the leader class is, you'll find its enemies,' he insisted.

'Me, for one,' I answered, 'if they call themselves that.'

But of course, he might be right. A residential town would be enough to turn anyone into a communist. I could live in the blackest industrial area, and never for a moment believe that revolution would make it any pleasanter; but long residence in any of the south-coast Blankmouths, full of folk with a sense of their own importance and nothing much to show for it, might make a communist of me in desperation.

'Anyway, if you want to burgle a desirable, pine-clad villa,' I said, 'you'll bloody well have to burgle it by yourself. And don't imagine for a moment that we're going to keep you out of quod.'

'You can go to hell, Taine,' he answered superbly. 'All I want from you is to pass on what I shall give you.'

As he paddled me back up the creek, I was convinced of the absolute futility of Pink. We were as silent and sullen as the brown water which had flooded the banks while we talked. I loathed the jargon which he used instead of thought. Would he ever understand, I wondered, that the proudest claim any man could make was to belong to the Servant Class? But of course, at bottom, he did. That was what was wrong with him and his former friends of the People's Union. They were ready enough to be Servants, but nobody wanted their services.

Nobody, nobody at all, wanted them. Oh, I don't know what it was which overwhelmed me with pity for the man – whether the motionless melancholy of Poole Harbour, or just his loneliness, which was emphasized, like that of some old maid, by the scrupulous neatness of his living-quarters.

However it was, I made one of those irrevocable remarks which change the course of a life. They are nearly always charitable remarks. One impulsively slaps someone else's burden on top of one's pack, and there it sticks for good. The irrevocable remark which destroys a relationship and eases one of responsibility for the neighbour as effectively as a kick in the face – well, that, too, stays for life, but on the conscience.

'Pink,' I said, 'what's the latest you can put me on shore?'

'Three hours from now.'

'Look here, if you care to take me back on board and spend those three hours telling your story – all of it, not just hints – I promise not to be hasty.'

'All of it?' he asked. 'I don't think you'd be much interested.'

'From your arrival in Portugal, I mean.'

'Oh . . . well, yes, I see your point.'

He swung the little pram round on her own axis, and paddled me back to *Olwen*. Till we were on board he didn't say a word except to mumble that there was plenty of gin.

I shall try not to put down anything that Pink did not tell me or imply, and I shall leave out his political asides. It is enough to say that he disliked socialists, communists and all other professional politicians, as well as Jews, Freemasons, Catholics, the Admiralty and the War Office. The only type of man that met with his approval was the chap selflessly doing a job in a Kiplingesque manner. Of this rare but admirable creature he felt that his own country had a monopoly, and that if foreigners and the masses could only be brought to see the value of him, the world might be run like a healthy public school.

You must imagine such a man standing on the waterfront of Lisbon with a valid passport, money enough, and some letters of introduction to friends whom he felt to be dubious. When he was organizing the rough stuff for the People's Union, he may have felt the romance of a movement which passed all frontiers – generally illegally – and he was quite at home with the bad characters of several nations. But he hadn't felt himself to be one of them. He was no internationalist, and he didn't much care for the society which was awaiting him.

He liked it a lot less that first night. After plenty of drinks and mutual commiseration, he came to anchor in a quiet restaurant with an Italian, a German and a Portuguese. They spoke German. It was Pink's only foreign language. He found it necessary to apologize to me for speaking it well. He had, he said, learned it – as a matter of duty – in the Navy.

Pink's reputation had preceded him; those letters of introduction, too, had been fulsome in praise of his audacity. Consequently the German and Italian felt free to talk. Their conversation played over the incidents of exile and after-war agitation – abortive plots, provoking of strikes, the personal weaknesses of intelligence officers, kidnappings to and from the Russian zones; and, as the red wine, for which the Portuguese was paying, slid down into their bellies, they were frank in discussion of ways for a bold man to earn his living on the fringes of politics. It shook Pink badly to see that these two comrades took him to be as ruthless a soldier of fortune as they. That wasn't his picture of himself at all. He was an English gentleman, exiled for the sake of his opinions.

The Portuguese had little to contribute beyond the drinks. He remained smiling and courteous, and, towards the end of the dinner, turned his attention exclusively to Pink. He assured him that Portugal was honoured by his presence, that he would have no trouble whatever with the authorities, and that if he, Pink, would obligingly keep an eye on British seamen and officers, and report from time to time . . .

'My God!' said Pink. 'He wanted me to be a copper's nark!'

He took credit for not smashing a plate on the secret policeman's head. Restraint of that sort he called tact.

In the weeks that followed, Pink, idly and morosely trailing between flashy bars and secretive cafés, began to appreciate where he stood. He did not doubt the idealism of his late leader, Heyne-Hassingham – and in that he was possibly right – but he had gained vision of the scum that every fascist wave carries along with it. He was far from admitting that he himself was part of that scum, but all the same he couldn't avoid some unpleasant hours of self-revelation.

A sensible man with Pink's private income, who couldn't return to his own country, would have bought himself a little sunny estate and settled down to a new life. Pink, however, couldn't keep out of mischief. His scheme for rehabilitating himself in his own eyes was to dive a bit deeper into the scum, with the vague intent of being on duty as a one-man secret service.

By this time he was well in with the Lisbon Germans. His particular friend was a certain Ritter, an ex-Nazi and former naval officer, of a far superior type to the German he had met on the evening of his arrival. Pink trusted him absolutely. They used to weep together over the Europe that might have been, if ever England and Germany had been allies, and they speculated happily on whether a communism in which the commissars were gentlemen might not be a very desirable state of affairs. Poor old Pink began to see himself in a double rôle – as saviour of the decent world by the force of this magnificent idea, and, at the same time, as Borer from Within.

He offered, of course, no problem at all to intelligent communist agents, who would have sized him up at once as a woolly and fearless character trying to cash in on the winning side when his own was doomed. They were quite willing that he should.

Ritter must have been chosen with considerable care to guide Pink along the way he should go. He put him to work as a courier to Italy. The job seemed natural enough to Pink; after all, he could travel freely – so long as he kept clear of territories under British control – and the German exiles could not. That he should be on friendly terms with ex-fascist communists in Milan, who were surprisingly easy to dine and drink with, did not disturb him. Wasn't it necessary to be an ally of communism in order to control it?

As soon as Pink had exhibited his remarkable facility for believing fairy-tales – and, I suppose, his talent for skulduggery of all sorts – his employers must have considered that he should be tied to them by more than loyalty. I needn't go into all the details of the sordid and complex story. Ritter filled him up with a bit of romance exactly calculated to appeal to Pink. He was to help in the rescue of a political prisoner who was being deported from Portugal.

Pink helped all right, but found himself alone in the night, on a country road, with a stolen taxi and a dead prisoner. He cleared out instantly and on foot – at the cost of leaving his finger-prints all over the dead man's baggage and the car. Ritter was full of apologies and explanations. He told Pink that he couldn't expect to play with fire without occasionally being burnt, and sent him over to Tangier to be out of the way.

Pink's life was becoming too complicated even for him. So, when he was offered the command, indeed the nominal ownership, of a neat little motor-cruiser that could do a hundred and fifty miles in one night, he refused. He was then reminded that if a set of his fingerprints, with his name and address at the bottom, were sent to the Portuguese police, he wouldn't be able to put up much of a defence. That was true. Pink didn't know who had fired that shot from the dark roadside, or why. He could only tell the jury the orders that Ritter had given him, and insist that he had been double-crossed. Ritter himself was out of reach. He had at last returned to East Germany and vanished.

'And if he ever comes out,' Pink shouted, 'I'll get him if I have to follow him for a month.'

I must admit that I found his longing for revenge somewhat over-dramatic and Italianate. I had still to learn that there are times when a man will kill as ruthlessly as in war, and with a hatred that is utterly unknown in war.

Well, Pink could do nothing but accept. The motor-cruiser's papers were in perfect order; and what more natural than that Pink, as a former naval officer under a cloud, should be living on a boat and idling away his time between Tangier and the fishing ports of Spain and Portugal? He was free to go on shore when he wished, visit hotels and amuse himself. When a job had to be done, his orders were brought to him by a Spaniard, who thereupon stayed on board, ostensibly as a paid hand. He was a good seaman, said Pink, and so discreetly cheerful a character that all embarrassment was avoided.

Meanwhile the one-man secret service was pretty well played out. Pink did not even know whether his employers were communists or Ritter's ambitious fellow-travellers or just a gang. What he was doing was plain enough – ferrying to and from North Africa people who did not wish their movements to be known. Often enough he was tempted to run into Gibraltar and throw himself on the mercy of naval intelligence officers.

'I wonder what would have happened,' he said to me, 'if I had just walked in and asked someone who knew me whether I was the sort of man to commit a cold-blooded murder.'

It was enough that he should wonder. In the bottom of his heart he knew quite well that his question would have been answered by a polite silence.

One day in early March his Spanish hand, spy or super-cargo – Pink never knew which he really was – came on board and gave him orders to proceed to Faro in Portugal, pick up a passenger, drop him in an inlet west of Cape Spartel, and take him back to Portugal the next night. Pink, who was then lying at Tangier, first went round the Cape to see what sort of place he was supposed to get into. His employers, he said, were no seamen. Weather and tide barely entered their calculations.

The inlet was only some ten miles from Tangier by land. There was a nasty sand-bar across the mouth, which was enough to discourage the curious, but could be crossed at the top of the tide provided the swell from the open Atlantic was not too heavy. The north bank of the inlet was obviously the property of a European. There were fields of lucerne, neatly wired, and a lot of paddocks and barns, with an attractive villa set above them on the terraced hillside. The estate looked like some sort of experimental station.

'Holberg's place, of course!' said Pink. 'He'd been working there since the early 1920s. I don't think anyone took him seriously. Tangier is too full of people with crazy hobbies.'

Pink and his Spaniard were conditioned by that time not to open their mouths for the discussion of anything more than navigation and what they would have for dinner. Some sort of explanation, however, couldn't be avoided. The Spaniard told him that a scientist who had been a refugee in Portugal and was now – like Ritter – returning to East Germany, was anxious to consult Holberg before he left, but had been refused a visa for Tangier. He added that Holberg had no politics at all – which agreed with all that Pink had heard about him.

'A surly sort of cove they called him in Tangier,' he told me, 'though he'd break out every so often and give a binge, and as likely as not be picked up stark naked a mile down the road.'

Well, Pink collected the eminent colleague without any trouble, put him ashore on Holberg's land and saw him escorted through the lucerne by a picturesque Berber servant in baggy pants. Pink and the Spaniard returned to their moorings in Tangier harbour, and set out the next evening to take the chap up again. He didn't come down to the creek at the appointed time, and after midnight, when there was only an hour left to catch the tide, Pink strolled up to the villa to see what was wrong.

He had a friendly chat with the Berber servant who was on guard in the patio between the wings of the house, and knew, of course, who he was. The Berber told him to go round to the front door, ring the bell and get the butler out of bed, and deliver his message.

'He had evidently got it in for the butler,' said Pink, 'but I didn't feel like obliging him.'

On his way round the house he passed the great east window of the living-room. The curtains were not drawn tight. He looked through; and there were the two Germans as drunk as students on a Saturday night, and happily gathered round a Christmas tree. His passenger kept passing a hand under the foliage and cackling with laughter. Then he would brush something off his hand into a tray beneath the tree.

Pink was interested. Since he had every right to be where he was, he could afford to take a chance of getting into the house, and possibly into the room, unseen. The plan of the room was inviting – at any rate to a rash lunatic such as Pink. On the side opposite the patio was a row of thick, low arches in the Spanish colonial style, and beyond them two doors into the entrance hall. If one of the doors opened quietly, he could enter the room unperceived by the occupants; if it didn't, he could always excuse himself on the grounds that he was looking for his passenger.

That villa, he said, was clean and fresh as a ship. Holberg evidently liked the night air of early spring to blow right through it. Pink accompanied the breeze through a window, and so into the entrance hall. The two doors into the long living-room were obvious. He chose one, slipped through and jumped behind a pillar. Pink, when he liked, could move like a scrum-half with leopard's paws for boots. I'd had experience of it.

He was in cover for the moment, but as soon as one of these boozing Germans got up to leave the room he had to be seen, single or double. There was nothing to hide him but a tall, tapestried chair in the corner of the room. He moved from pillar to pillar, and so to chair. He described himself as being perfectly safe behind it. It wouldn't occur to him that he might sneeze, or that someone might want the chair. He wasn't blessed with that sort of imagination.

Holberg and passenger were certainly taking their hair down over the bottles. They had reverted to the noisy indiscretions of youth. That, evidently, was Holberg's form of relaxation: to drink himself riotous once a month or so with some chosen companion. The passenger was just the man for him – it was probable that they had known each other at the university – and they were having fun with heavy technical jokes that weren't at all easy to understand. Indeed, they were having fun at the expense of everything but themselves, the communist party included. It was frankly assumed between them that they had joined the party because it offered the only hope of revenge on the brother – yes, they called them brother-Anglo-Saxons.

Then the Christmas tree came in for more attention. Now that Pink could observe it more closely, he saw that it wasn't a tree, but branches of some North African thorn standing in a big vase, or, perhaps, potted in earth. It pleased the passenger to baptize the leaves of the thorn with wine and to giggle because something – Pink didn't know the word he used – was remarkably resistant to alcohol.

After a bit they reached a solemn and tearful state of mutual admiration. Pink's passenger stood up and made a set speech to his colleague in imitation of a chancellor or public orator conferring high honours upon him. The missing word, now repeated in several contexts, was clear. The things on the thorn which the passenger had attracted to his hand and baptized with wine were cattle ticks.

Now, anyone who listens to a foreign language spoken rapidly by two drunks with a heap of slurred technicalities and private allusions isn't going to get a lot of the sense. Pink admitted that even if he had been a vet he couldn't have given a detailed account of what he overheard; he claimed, however, to be sure of the main facts. That well-lubricated passenger had run on and on with so many repetitions that he often gave a second chance at his meaning.

It was clear that Holberg had been working for years on an anti-toxin for foot-and-mouth disease, and had managed to establish the virus in a strain of cattle ticks. The tick was none the worse; and, if removed from an infected cow when swollen with blood, it could be brewed up by some process or other, and the anti-bodies extracted from the mash. Pink's passenger was congratulating Holberg on his discovery of a prophylactic against the disease.

That was not all. These little specks, poised on the outer tips of the thorn branches, ready to fall on the outstretched hand or any other convenient feeding-ground which passed beneath them, transmitted the virus from one to another, and increased its activity in the procession. Holberg's ticks, dead, gave immunity; alive, they gave a most malignant form of the disease. Pink's passenger digressed into a mock dissertation on the wonders of nature, using an empty bottle as pointer towards an imaginary blackboard.

Holberg, at last a little bored by all this academic rowdiness, opened another bottle as an encouragement to his colleague to sit down. They started to talk personalities, always in a spirit of bitterness.

'You know how some chaps throw things about when they've got a skinful,' said Pink. 'And I like busting a bit of crockery myself so long as I'm among friends. Well, these fellows threw words instead.'

They said what they thought of the Russian scientists to whom Holberg's process of immunization was to be passed, and circled the rest of the world with abuse. Their respect was confined to themselves and the ticks. Any fool, it appeared, could handle ticks; they were obliging enough to stay alive and wait for the chance of a meal wherever there were reasonable warmth and shade.

The two Germans lowered their voices, and the next remark that Pink heard distinctly was from his passenger.

'You're out of date, dear doctor! Out of date! The English are only poor Europeans like the rest of us now. Gone are the days when they could just order more meat from the Argentine.'

This made Pink particularly angry. That those days *were* gone was exactly what he resented. He was frank enough to admit to me that he could concentrate on nothing but how to smash the pair of them up and get away with it, and that he missed a vital bit of conversation.

When he had ceased to see red, he heard Holberg ask:

'Is he a communist?'

'As much as you and I. He believes that only through the Russians can we Germans rule the world.'

'You're sure he can't go wrong?'

'He'll have full instructions,' the passenger replied, 'and he's a competent entomologist who has lived in England for years.'

Pink waited for more, but the two drifted off into what he called beastly biological obscenities. Pink was too well brought up to appreciate two drunken scientists on the subject of sex.

He looked at his watch. He had been in the room nearly an hour, and it was very possible that his Spaniard would come up from the creek to see what had happened to him, or that the Berber servant in the patio would think it suspicious that he had not returned.

Pink's luck was in. Holberg lurched over to the window, with some trite remark to the effect that God's good air was better than plumbing, and the passenger followed suit. While they were so satisfactorily engaged, Pink nipped out the way he had come, and went round to the front door and rang the bell.

Almost at once Holberg himself opened the door. The man was quite fearless, Pink said. It may, of course, have been the wine, but the general impression Holberg made on him – and he had seen him sober – was couldn't-care-less-if-I-die-tomorrow. Pink apologized for disturbing him, saying that he had been ringing for some time and had not been able to make anyone hear. He explained the need to catch the tide. Holberg blasted the tide, and laid it down that his guest was going to stay the night. Pink made himself as pleasant as possible, for he wanted to be invited in for a drink, and said that of course the tide didn't matter if Holberg could ensure the passenger coming on board without being seen by any curious eyes.

Pink must have been at the top of his form during this doorstep interview, and really exercising self-control. Holberg gave him a drink, using another room, and there the Spaniard found him, jabbering away on excellent terms with Holberg and the passenger. They weren't in any state to distinguish one half hour from another, and Pink was perfectly safe unless the Spaniard exchanged exact information with the Berber servant – which, naturally, he did not.

The passenger came on board in the early afternoon, and slept till dusk, when they were swooping over the long swell to Portugal. He joined Pink in the wheelhouse, and began to question him about the appearance of Southern England, which he had never seen – but evidently knew well from books and maps.

'Not much forest?' he asked. 'Not as we know forest in Germany?'

Pink agreed.

'And the New Forest. It is nearly all cut – no?'

Pink told him that in these days there was more heath than woodland, but still a good many miles of trees. The conversation was beginning to interest him. To hide his excitement he played the conscientious man at the wheel, and kept staring north-west into the night.

The passenger wanted to know what was the town most handy to the New Forest, and Pink said it was Southampton.

'Not Bournemouth?'

'Well, Bournemouth would do as well.'

'And the downs? How do they look, the downs? Is there nothing but grass?'

Pink told him of the hanging woods, the bracken and the furze.

'Oak, ash and thorn, eh?' said the passenger with a slight sneer.

I don't suppose he was ever nearer to death than at that moment. Pink was sentimental as any other exile, and he was boiling with anger and suspicion. But he would have had to put the Spaniard overboard, too; and he couldn't bear the thought of his only comrade – spy though he might be – shouting in the creamy wash until he was hidden by the night.

'Hawthorn and blackthorn,' he answered deliberately. 'Brakes of them and thick hedges of them.'

'And Bournemouth is near this downland, too?'

'Good enough,' said Pink.

The passenger seemed content. He chattered away patronizingly through most of the night until they landed him at the rendezvous east of Faro, but didn't say another word that was any use to Pink.

'Now that's all I have,' Pink admitted to me very honestly. 'But, by God, isn't it enough?'

I put on a decent semblance of interest, but I couldn't agree for a moment that it was enough. What did it all boil down to? That an unreliable, unbalanced semi-gangster had, or said he had, overheard the alcoholic extravagances of two German biologists. Pink was too anxious to rehabilitate himself – and the very type to read into anything he heard just what he wanted to hear.

If I were to stretch a point in his favour, and believe that his report was accurate, I might assume that one of these days we should learn that there wasn't any more foot-and-mouth disease behind the Iron Curtain, and that proletarian science had scored another triumph; but the evidence of any plot to use the disease as a cold war weapon was of the slimmest.

Still, I hadn't heard the whole story yet; and as the rest of it came hesitatingly from his bearded mouth, I couldn't help being impressed by the fact that he had gone nap on his so-called information. He was risking his liberty and probably his life because he believed in the truth of his own deductions.

Between voyages Pink had been left pretty much to himself, for it was essential that he should keep up the appearance of a harmless idler. He was even permitted to take short cruises on his own, so long as he let the Spaniard know where he was going and what his ports of call would be. So, after their last job, Pink told him that he thought of running down the Moroccan coast to Mogador.

As soon as the Spaniard had left, Pink filled the cabin with cans of petrol, and deliberately put out from Tangier into a threat of foul weather blowing up from the west. He was told from right and left that it was folly, and that he would never be seen again. That was what he wanted to be told, as publicly as possible.

Once clear of the land, he turned north and ran six hundred miles to Vigo, where he took on more fuel. He didn't tell me much about that voyage except to say that it was odd how a man could fight for his life when he didn't care whether he died or not.

He cleared out of Vigo, with the weather moderating, and steered north-west across the Bay of Biscay. The Bay was in a kindly mood, and he let his boat drift, he said, and slept for twelve hours. He meant to pick up the Brittany coast at night, sink his ship and get ashore without being seen; it would then be assumed that he was, as he deserved to be, at the bottom of the Atlantic. He didn't think that his call at Vigo was likely to be traced. Vigo was far outside the normal range of his craft, and he had been alongside the fuelling wharf and out again in one dull and menacing evening without ever passing through customs or harbour office.

Disappearance, however, wasn't so easy, for his dinghy had been smashed by the gale beyond repair. He had no means of getting ashore. He solved the problem by lashing together a raft of empty petrol cans and gratings, upon which he paddled himself and two suitcases into the Bay of Morbihan. He walked through the night to Vannes, took an early west-bound train, and by the afternoon was nothing but a casual Englishman enjoying a holiday in Brittany.

In a little Breton port he bought the sardine boat that was now *Olwen*. He had her converted by a local yard, and put in a powerful Diesel and extra tanks. I gathered that for six weeks, while his beard grew and his hands were busy with plane and chisel, he was further from romantic impatience than he had ever been.

'I'd like to go shares in a little yard,' he said, 'if ever . . . You don't know a country where there's no extradition, do you?'

In *Olwen*, still nameless, he disappeared again, carrying

gallons of paint as cargo, and didn't touch land until he was safe in the Essex marshes. There, next morning, he was a normal unit of the local population – a casual and seemingly ignorant yachtsman, who had just brought his boat round from London and was painting her up ready for the season on a remote hard.

'Then I went to see Roland,' he said. 'I knew of him from People's Union days. I'd always heard he was a nasty piece of work, and he is. I see his position, of course – still, he might have had common courtesy. He just said my information was unconvincing. It probably was. I didn't get a chance to spread myself. You can't tell a piece of your life to a bastard who's plain hostile. God, he made a favour of not handing me over to the police! I told him he could go to hell if he'd just answer one question – how was a chap to set about it, if he wanted to find out who were the authorities on insects in a given town? He dealt with that one quick as a flash. I should go to the Public Library and get out all the books on local bugs and look puzzled; as soon as the librarian was interested, I was to tell him I'd found a blue centipede or something and couldn't identify it, and he'd be sure to put me in touch with the blokes who could.'

'And it worked?' I asked.

'Oh, yes, it worked. I tucked myself away in this anchorage, and through the Bournemouth librarian I got hold of an old codger in a backstreet, with drawers full of dusty beetles, who was secretary of the local bug-hunting society. I couldn't talk his patter, but I saw from a notice on his desk that he was secretary of the local spiritualists too. Well, my mother was always turning tables and that sort of thing, so I was on a good wicket. I came away with a load of happy pamphlets and a short list of people who might identify my centipede. Schoolteachers, retired Indian Army, and so forth. You could rule 'em all out straight away – except one, a Dr Losch, who used to address the society from time to time. Refugee from Nazi Germany. Aryan. The usual thing. In 1940 we ran him in, and in 1942 we let him out again with apologies. Well, that's the man.'

'Damn it, Pink,' I said, 'how in the world do you know he is?'

'Watched him. Climbed a pine-tree with some sandwiches and spent a whole day watching him. And what's more, I'm not the only person watching him. There's a kind of writer chap, typing away in a window opposite Losch's drive, where he can keep an eye on all his visitors.'

'Couldn't he be just staring out of the window?' I asked.

'What for? And I found out that Losch has got a laboratory on the second floor. I could see a bit of white tile when the door was opened, and he was hopping in and out with glass measures and things.'

'One would expect him to have a bathroom,' I suggested mildly.

'Oh, to hell with you! One can tell the difference. I tell you he's the sort of man Holberg and my passenger would know. He's a competent bug-hunter. And he lives in Bournemouth. What more do you want?'

'It's his house you intend to burgle?'

'Yes. And I'm going to find ticks.'

'But if you do, they aren't evidence of anything.'

'No? If I shove 'em on a cow, and the wretched cow keels over a week later, and if somebody then raids Holberg, isn't that evidence?'

Well, I could see that there was nothing for it but burglary, from Pink's point of view, if he cared to take the risk. Roland couldn't go breaking into private houses. As for the police, they would be delighted if Pink called on them, and would advise him, with that grim kindliness of theirs, not to stick to so preposterous a story before the judge. I mentally damned Pink, Bournemouth and myself – for being a fool – but I did feel that I should have an uneasy conscience if I refused to be drawn in.

'Look here!' said Pink, seeing that I was wavering. 'I heard the voices of those two swine and you didn't, so I don't blame you for doubting. But do this much for me. Hang about while I bust in. Just pretend you're waiting for your girl or something – you're a respectable citizen, and you'll get away with it. And it's all as easy as kiss-my-hand. I know the cop's beat, and I've found a way in through the coal cellar.'

We fixed up the rough details for an attempt the following night, which was Thursday. When Pink rowed me ashore for the second time, I felt towards him – well, not yet liking, but at least a godfatherly, colonelish interest in his well-hidden virtues.

Before going home, I drove into the outskirts of Bournemouth and through the streets around Losch's house. The district was pleasantly laid out in curving, leafy roads, with small patches of natural woodland; and the houses must have been built in the early twentieth century when even a retired shopkeeper could afford to cut himself off from neighbours by a considerable extent of garden. Thus there was no lack of cover, and I felt sure that I could come and go undetected.

I had no intention of being more than an observer. I was prepared to hold a watching brief for Roland – without, of course, compromising him by a single word – and to be a witness, if a witness were ever necessary, to the fact that Pink had really entered the house he claimed to have entered. It was understood, however, that Pink and I in the presence of any third person simply didn't know each other.

I explained this to Cecily, emphasizing that I ran no risk

whatever. She wasn't impressed. She didn't like the entanglement at all.

'But you do see I couldn't refuse?' I insisted. 'Pink behaved very well, and it wasn't much to ask.'

'Roland hadn't any right to bring you in,' she said.

She ignored Pink altogether. She loathed the thought of him, of course. I knew, however, that my account of him must have aroused all her ready pity, though she was determined to give no sign of it.

I answered weakly that I liked the tradition of voluntary service.

'What about all the time you put in lecturing to Women's Institutes?' I asked.

'It isn't the same,' she said. 'All Roland's work should be done by people who are paid by the government.'

'With pensions for the widows?'

That was self-defence. My conscience was uneasy, for I suspected that she was just right, and I wasn't admitting it. But I should have been just as discontented with myself if I had refused to help Pink.

'I hate it when you say things like that,' she cried, as if I had deliberately hurt her. 'Why *must* you do it?'

This was a conversation which we should have laughed over afterwards. Mere differences of words, of opinions, never bothered us for long; for, in the end, the underlying cause always turned out to be a clash between two different aspects of our love for each other. But, on this occasion, the atmosphere was just perceptibly cool when I left for the office in the morning. We never had time to make it clear that neither of us was saying what was meant; and so, later, we wildly exaggerated the incident until each of us was obstinately believing things which had never been said at all.

I dined in Bournemouth and went to a movie, and at eleven met Pink in the pine trees opposite Losch's house. He looked a villainous figure in dark-blue blouse and trousers, with black canvas shoes and thin black gloves. Slung over his shoulder was one of those black-japanned metal cases used by collectors of plants – a vasculum, I believe it is called. The handle of a saw was sticking out of one of his blouse pockets, and he was bulging all over with odd tools and a couple of torches. There was also a familiar-shaped bulge at his hip. We had a bitter argument about it in low voices. Eventually I got the gun off him.

He told me that he had taken *Olwen* out into the harbour, and that she now lay at anchor off The Haven. The pram, in which he had come ashore, was on a bit of beach not far from the old flying-boat station. If he had to run for it, he intended to go straight for the pram and return on board. If he got clear away, with or without results, he would meet me at my car which was parked in another quiet road half a mile away.

Losch's property was on a corner site. The front of the house was separated from the main residential road by a short, well-gravelled drive. This eastern side, said Pink, was to be avoided at all costs; the gravel crunched under the lightest of steps, and the drive was overlooked by the house across the road, where he claimed to have seen a man with a typewriter staring out of the window.

On the two interior sides, south and west, the garden was surrounded by a six-foot brick wall, with broken glass on top, suggesting that some previous owner had disliked his neighbour's children. The north side, flanking a second residential street, was divided from the pavement by a stiff hedge and shrubbery. Across the street was the coppice of pine trees where we were.

'I'll show you your station,' said Pink. 'Up after me, and no noise!'

He led me up a pine with conveniently spaced branches.

Perched securely some twenty-five feet above the ground, we could see the whole northern side of the house and quite a bit of the front. Opposite us, beyond the shrubbery, was a flower-bed and then a flagged kitchen yard where was the door of Pink's coal cellar. He had been inside earlier in the week, and found that the second door, which led from the cellar into the house, had a lock which could easily be cut clean out.

Otherwise it was a house that would have been thoroughly approved by the police. The downstairs doors and windows were solid, and carefully locked. Indeed, we saw Losch and a manservant methodically checking and closing them all. Then we watched the chequer-board of lights winking on and off upstairs, and followed the routine of a respectable house putting itself to sleep. It seemed to be inhabited only by Losch and a married couple.

After midnight Pink swung himself down to earth like some bearded tar of the days of sail, and slipped away beneath the trees. I saw him nip across the road into the garden next to Losch's. He preferred the wall with its broken glass to the longish process of pushing through a hedge on a road that was too long, too straight and too well lighted.

From my tree I had a clear view of the tidy ribbon of street, the hedge and the kitchen yard. The wind was blowing up from the south-west, and the branches began to fan back and forth. After a quarter of an hour the local cop strolled down the road and flashed his light into the grove where I was. I watched that confounded beam in terror lest it should lift, but fortunately he was searching for indecent behaviour rather than burglar's mates. As soon as he had passed on, I saw Pink glide along the doors of the kitchen yard and disappear into one of them. I listened, but I couldn't hear his tools at work. The only sounds for long minutes were the shriek of a little owl, who saw and disapproved of me, and the distant movement of heavy lorries far away in the centre of Bournemouth.

The dark block swallowed Pink and slept on, presenting to me walls of absolute, blank negation. Never have I had so disturbing an impression of the European house. From the moment that the builder has hung the front door and put in the black glass of windows, no one can know – I mean know, not imagine – what goes on within. A house is impenetrable as a man, and its eyelessness more uncanny.

Between the flicking of the tossed branches I thought I saw a finger of light stab into one of the downstairs rooms. If it were really there, it meant that Pink had emerged from the basement and was on his way up. I was confident that he wasn't as nervous as I. Yet how could he be sure that he wouldn't trip over something? How on earth could he know that one of the three people in the house was not awake and listening? Sitting safely in my pine, I couldn't imagine a viler way of making a living than burglary. It must, I suppose, have a damnable fascination. After all there is no other skilled civilian craft which can be exercised in a state of wild excitement.

My heart pumped intolerably – no other action being open to it – when I saw, this time quite clearly, a tiny pool of light on the floor of the bedroom which we believed to be Losch's. Through the open door of that room Pink had caught his glimpse of a sunlit passage and of the white tiles beyond, which, he would have it, didn't belong to a bathroom.

I could guess what he was doing – checking his position in the house, so that he could go straight to the door he wanted. He would now be tiptoeing over to the south side of which we knew next to nothing, and far from the illusory safety of the familiar face of brick. I looked at my watch and found it was nearly one. Pink was taking his time over the job with professional patience.

Another ten minutes passed. Then that house burst into life with the violence of an old Bournemouth spinster finding a man under her bed. There was a crash that I could hear from my tree – muffled by walls, but still an unmistakable, calamitous crash. Two front windows were suddenly illuminated. A voice cried *Sir! Sir!* Losch's light went on, and I saw him grab his dressing-gown and something from the bedside drawer which might have been a gun. I heard a yell, and heavy footsteps drumming on the stairs. All the ground floor windows were flooded with light. The front door flew open. Losch appeared on the steps, shouting for police and blowing a whistle. Then the cop came pounding up the road and round the corner, also blowing a whistle, and dashed into the house with Losch.

There was still no sign of Pink. Where in God's name, I cursed, was he? And what was I to do? I didn't dare climb higher into the tree in case I couldn't get down in time, and I didn't dare to take to the ground in case I couldn't get up in time. I can never remember being in such a disgraceful state of dither.

Then at last I saw Pink jump at the downstairs window opposite me with a heavy dining-room chair for battering-ram. The window fell out on the flagged yard with a smash that must have been heard a mile away. He followed, dived over the hedge, parting the top of it like a horse through the brushwood of a steeplechase jump, and landed on his hands. He kicked his feet clear, and charged across the road into the pines. His figure was extraordinary; it flashed through my mind that his back must have been broken in a struggle. Then I saw him hauling the vasculum out of his blouse; it was that which had given him his pigeon-breasted appearance. Without a word he dropped it at the foot of my tree, bolted back on to the road and started to sprint down it with the cop and Losch's manservant after him.

A black police car shrieked round that respectable corner and joined in the chase. Pink saw or heard it in time, and vanished from the road. The police were out of the car and after him in five seconds, but my money was on Pink. I felt that through heath and gardens he could reach, somewhere, the water of Poole Harbour without ever showing himself for more than the swift crossing of a road.

There was wild excitement around my corner. All the little, well-bred terriers of the district were yapping their heads off and pretending they had noticed something wrong before the human beings. In half a dozen houses the lights were on, and somewhere a woman was having hysterics in the same key as the smaller dogs. Still, nobody had ventured out into the road, and it was evident that this was the moment to pick up the vasculum. I slid down to the ground and grabbed it.

My next move had to be decided on the instant. Anyone walking away ran a risk of being stopped by police and asked politely where he had been – and I hadn't got the shadow of an excuse for walking through streets that didn't lead anywhere at quarter past one in the morning. On the other hand, if I stayed where I was, I must chance a search of the coppice by the police.

I compromised and tried to get clear of all those desirable but very noisy residences without leaving cover. It couldn't be done. The pines extended over a mere couple of acres in the shape of a triangle. Houses or walls forced me on to one road or the other. No doubt, if I had been Pink, I should have gone on regardless of walls; but the last thing I wanted was to be caught stumbling through somebody's private property on such a night. So, sticking feebly to my legal right to be on common land, I plunged into a clump of massive

41

rhododendrons on the edge of the eastern road. They were old enough and strong enough for me to stand uncomfortably between two forks a few feet off the ground.

I was only just in time. Bournemouth police went through that coppice like a dose of methodical salts. They couldn't, of course, be sure that the escaped burglar had an accomplice, but, if he had, that bit of cover was the place for him. They found with ease that very climbable tree, marked by our shoes and those of uncountable boys, and they sent an active young detective up it. That gave them the idea of flashing lights into the tops of all the trees – as well as on the ground under the bushes. They had a quick look at my rhododendrons, but since I was, as it were, in the middle air, they missed me. While the puddle of light crept below my feet, I found myself using the most obscene mental language against the guiltless Roland, not against Pink – thereby coming into line with my absent and anxious Cecily.

At two, when all was clear and the residents of that select district had returned to bed, I ventured out and slunk rapidly down the road, with the strap of the vasculum over my shoulder. My imagination, violently stimulated in the rhododendrons, had produced a possible story for anyone who asked me to account for myself. I was going to say that I had been out catching moths.

I turned a couple of corners and then walked, trying to remember that I was a citizen confident of his innocence, straight along the pavement to the lot, some four hundred yards away, where I had parked my car. When I came to a bright street lamp I stopped, rather abruptly and without forethought, to satisfy my curiosity about the possible contents of the vasculum. This unexpected halt caught my follower on the wrong foot. I heard his steps and looked round. He did his best to appear to be casually crossing the road. I didn't open the vasculum, and pretended to be looking at my watch. There was nothing more that I or the unknown could do without arousing mutual suspicion, so on we walked, he about fifty yards behind me and now on the other side of the road.

I was half-way to safety and my car when I met a solitary constable. I wished him good night in what I hoped was a cultured and respectable tone, and he was, I think, going to pass on after a sharp scrutiny when a voice shouted with surprising authority:

'Constable, stop that man!'

There was nothing to be gained by bolting, so I smiled at the cop and said that, Good Lord, I hoped I hadn't been trespassing or anything.

My follower came running up. He had a sharp, unshaven face and a muffler tucked untidily into his waistcoat. He looked, to my relief, a bit woolly and intellectual. The police don't like that sort; they have a mildly Hellenic idea that the just man should also be beautiful. I had little doubt that the word of a decent and innocent business-man would be taken against the stranger's.

'I live opposite Dr Losch's house,' he said with a keen precision, 'which has just been broken into. I saw this man leaving the trees across the road in a suspicious manner. I wish you to question him.'

'What trees? I've been in a lot of trees,' I protested indignantly. 'I've been watching moths.'

'May I have your name and address, sir?' asked the policeman with judicial neutrality.

I gave it him, together with my business card and some odd letters in my pocket.

'That's quite all right, sir. And might I see what you have in that there tin case?'

I opened it with a silent prayer that Pink had laid off Dr Losch's silver. There was nothing inside but a few twigs of thorn. The thorn wasn't like any English thorn that I knew. In the semi-darkness I couldn't see whether the twigs were inhabited.

Pink's success swung me straight into a fighting mood. I don't mean that I wanted – far from it! – any sort of depressing violence. I do mean that all motives, all doubtings of conscience, were cleared up. I could have faced a general, even the angriest of them.

'That's quite all right, sir,' the constable said. 'And perhaps you would tell me where you're for now.'

'Back to my car. A grey saloon parked just off the road two hundred yards on. You may have noticed it as you came along.'

'I am very sorry to have troubled you,' the stranger said to me, with a slight roll of his r's, 'and you too, constable.'

'That's quite all right, sir,' the cop replied – his continual, unmoved *all rights* reminded me of an unintelligent father comforting his children. 'Our job would be a sight easier if all the public was as helpful. Now you're one as notices things, and if you could remember seeing the *right* man . . .'

'You know what he looks like?' the stranger interrupted eagerly.

'The man as the police would like to interview, sir, is —' He opened his notebook and refreshed his memory. 'Height about six feet. Build, stronganactive. Brown beard. Nose been broken. Wearing dark-blue battle-dress or garment resembling the same. Might be a seaman.'

'Nose broken,' repeated the stranger. 'Is anything known of his politics?'

'He didn't hardly stop long enough to have a friendly chat,' the policeman grinned.

He said good night, and moved on into the dark and obedient road. The stranger walked along with me towards my car, apologizing fulsomely and making it appear that he accompanied me merely because he could not bring himself to stop talking. I wasn't in the least afraid of him; indeed, I wanted him to give some more of himself away. That question of his about Pink's politics was so utterly unEnglish. As if anyone could know what were the politics of a burglar! It looked to me as if the question had been automatic – which well it might be, if my inquisitive friend had had any police training behind the Iron Curtain.

He tried to entangle the conversation in moths, but I wasn't having any. I just said that the lepidoptera of towns were a most interesting study, and passed on to simulated enthusiasm over the trees and gardens of Bournemouth.

So we came to the car. He stood talking, evidently reluctant to let me go without a clearer personal impression of me. The facts he had already – my name, my home and business addresses, and the number of my car. I gossiped away as if I loved the man, for I held all the cards. With every moment I was growing more suspicious of him, and he, as he listened to my prattlings of wife and family, had less reason to be suspicious of me. I even offered to run him home, if he would tell me where was this Dr Losch about whom all the fuss had been and to whom, he said, he lived opposite.

No, he couldn't think of it. And we were standing by the car, arguing with warm politeness about whether he would take a lift or not, when Pink charged out of the bushes and caught the man a clip on the side of the head that knocked him flat in the road.

'What the hell do you think you're doing?' I shouted, as if I'd never seen Pink before in my life. 'By God, it's the chap the policeman described!'

Pink stood there, hesitant, with an air of raging stupidity as of some brute of a dog which has just attacked the postman and been called to order.

The stranger raised himself on one elbow, and coolly flashed a light on Pink's face.

'The Portuguese police would like him, too,' he said.

I think that was no more than an inspired guess – on the evidence of the twisted nose and the opportunity that Pink, if he were still alive, might have had of penetrating Holberg's secrets – by a man who had stored in his professional memory every single relevant fact.

Pink's face showed that the shot had gone home; also he dropped his hand to the pocket where his gun ought to have been and, as I then thanked God, was not.

The stranger turned his back on us and walked steadily away. It must have been obvious to him that, whoever I was, I wanted to avoid a scandal, and that this was the moment to extricate himself. But he was certainly putting a courageous trust in English law and order.

'You blazing, bloody idiot!' I hissed at Pink. 'What on earth did you do that for?'

'Damn you! He's the chap with the typewriter who watches Losch's house,' he answered furiously.

'Well, what of it?'

'God, Taine! Do you think that after all that trouble I'd let him force his way into your car and get the case back?'

I explained, choking with forced patience, that I was trying to persuade him to get in, and that he hadn't the slightest suspicion of me.

'Well, how could I know, with half a gale blowing from me to you?' he roared. 'Lord, man, I was thinking of the country, not your politenesses!'

'Pink, the trouble with you is that you hit first and think afterwards,' I said, 'country or not. For God's sake, shave off that beard and change your clothes and get out of Poole Harbour tonight. Where will I find you?'

He stormed some more to cover his misery. And misery it was – though I doubt if I had realized then that Pink knew when he had made a fool of himself as quickly as anyone else.

'I'll go round to West Bay,' he grumbled. 'I've kept pretty quiet up the harbour, and there's lots of beards about. It'll take the police a few days to get on to the chap who was living in *Olwen,* and by that time your fellow Roland will be able to call 'em off.'

He looked hard at me, as if trying to find enough friendliness left in my eyes for him to sink his pride and ask a favour.

'Get him to give me a break over that Portuguese business if he can.'

I assured him curtly that of course I would, and that everything possible would be done for him if the ticks proved the truth of his story. Then I said goodbye. Poor Pink! I wonder how many times in his life he had been within reach of astounding success, and then had to listen to some commanding officer – or mere associate, such as I – blistering him with contempt and anger.

Even there at the roadside I could see what disastrous complications he had introduced into the beautiful simplicity of his raid. He had not only wrecked his own clever and heroic effort to prove his own death, but he had given away the reason why Losch's house had been entered, and warned at least one interested party. Whatever the reason why the stranger watched the house, he couldn't have known that it had been broken into for any purpose but plain theft. His attitude both to me and to the policeman had shown that he was consumed by curiosity, utterly in the dark, and had not even recognized the contents of the vasculum for what they were.

When I left Pink, I drove straight home. I can't blame

myself for that decision. I wanted to see Cecily and assure her that all was well. I also wanted to telephone my clerk when he turned up at the office at nine, and tell him what to do about my appointments and how to excuse my absence. It was a perfectly natural decision for the father of a family with a one-man business. There was no point in charging off to Roland then and there. I wasn't afraid of anything the stranger could do. I didn't think he was likely to set the police on me, and, if he did, I should have no difficulty in persuading any of my acquaintances at County Headquarters to accompany me and the vasculum to London, and hear the truth of the story.

I got home soon after three, dragged Cecily out of bed to join me in a drink she didn't want, and had a look at the contents of the vasculum in a good light. The thorn twigs were well inhabited; there was a score of little black and motionless dots under and on the tips of the leaves. Cecily was rather silent. She tried to echo my note of triumph – for I did feel that I had reason to be proud of my belief in Pink – but she didn't sound quite real. Like many women who are by nature guarded and thoughtful, her true opinion is to be found not in what she says, but in the inflexions of her voice when she says it.

'Why didn't you go to Roland straight away?' she asked.

'I wanted to see you,' I answered.

'You should have thought of that earlier,' she said.

It was an obscure remark, but it made me feel guilty. During the war she was a model Spartan wife. In time of peace, however, avoidable anxiety is not fair.

I slept heavily and late. She, I gathered, did not; for she told me in the morning that three cars, or the same car three times, had passed our house just before dawn. That was, indeed, a rare event on our country road, but I wasn't, or refused to be impressed. I considered it quite possible that the stranger, thanks to Pink, had come early from Bournemouth to have a look at my house, and what of it? After all we were in well-policed England, and this time – unlike that very unpleasant night the previous autumn when I was on the run – the police would be on my side.

Cecily took Jerry and George to school in the village. After that she was going to see the vicar – for some reason it is impossible in the country to indulge in any normal community activity without seeing the vicar – so she said goodbye until the evening. I finished my bacon and eggs, and then picked up the telephone to call my office and to make an appointment with Roland. The line was dead.

I went outside to see if the wire from my house to the pole had been interfered with. It hadn't. Then I remembered that the night had been blustery, and I declined to be affected by Cecily's mood of foreboding. The line, after all, went dead at least once a year. It passed under half a mile of chestnuts which were always drooping their heavy branches over it, in spite of the work of the Post Office linesmen and their saws.

There was no point in driving up to the village just to find that all the lines, and not only mine, were down; so I set out for Dorchester. I was cautious, but not at all convinced that I had any reason to be. I reckoned that if my telephone had really been cut by some crazy outfit, normally inhabiting the world of Pink, their only purpose was to gain time to escape. The game was up for them, and any strong-arm stuff would merely set the whole machinery of the police in action. I took only one precaution, and that was to unload Pink's gun in case I had to frighten someone with it.

I also intended to drive pretty fast, but that I could not do. Half a mile from my house I caught up a plain, dusty black van which would not let me pass. Even this was not conclusive. On our twisting roads a slow and nervous driver can hold up the car behind him for bend after bend. Then the van stopped in the middle of the road and spilled out two men from the double doors at the back.

They darted straight at my car. I was out of it on the instant, and held them up with Pink's gun. They gave me no trouble. I was a bit of an expert in house-to-house fighting towards the end of the war, and for a naturally peaceful man I can put on a convincing show of ferocity. These two chaps were well-trained, too. They kept their hands up, and their eyes on my face without flickering off for a moment; and that, since another couple were creeping up behind me, must have been difficult.

The spacing of the attack was perfect. The other two had been hiding behind the hedge just round the corner of an open gate. I had only just time to half-turn my head when my arms were grasped, and a pad of some anaesthetic forced over my face. There was so little chance to put up an effective struggle that I wasn't even hurt beyond a few bruises. My arms and legs were securely held, and the more I heaved, the more I inhaled that damned chloroform mixture.

When I recovered consciousness I was on the floor of the van, neatly tied up and fairly comfortably settled on a pile of sacking. I don't think I had been laid out for more than a few minutes, for I felt well enough after all the vivid dreams had cleared away. The stranger from Bournemouth and another man were with me. They had the vasculum. I decided that there was nothing whatever to be gained by anger or protest.

'How the devil do you think you are going to get away with this?' I asked as reasonably as I could manage. 'You aren't in Russia, you know.'

'In Russia there is fortunately no need for this violence,' the stranger answered.

Well, I suppose he was right. The population must be even more law-abiding than in England. They'd better be.

'But, my dear sir,' I told him, 'my office, my wife, everybody will be looking for me.'

'Naturally! And so I shall not keep you more than a few hours.'

'You'll have the police after you before that.'

'It is possible,' he replied with a half-smile that held in it a weary fatalism. 'But you did not want to appeal to the police last night, and I do not think you can have done so since.'

'And what about my car?'

'That? That has been driven away. I needed it. I will explain to you later.'

It is curious how one attaches quite a different meaning to the same face according to the circumstances in which one sees it. I had first thought of this man as fussy and eager and considering himself too intelligent for Bournemouth. Then, as we walked together to my car, I put him down as some grubby sort of foreign agent. Now I saw that he was a man of a certain melancholy power, as cool and concentrated as some professional bridge-player calculating how far his poor hand can be used to wreck his opponents. Yet all the time I was looking at the same face, with its sharp nose and thin mouth, and eyes set exceptionally close together so that his gaze focused for exact clarity of the object before him, to the exclusion of all vaguer shadows at the side.

His real name I do not know. His assistants addressed him, with considerable respect, as Yegor Ivanovitch. That Russian custom of using the patronymic instead of the surname must be most useful in revolutionary circles. From the moment I woke up in the van he never made any attempt to hide the fact that he was a Russian security officer. Indeed, he had every interest in letting me know it. We were, from his point of view, unwilling allies.

I lay on the sacking for about three-quarters of an hour of fairly fast driving. We passed through no big town. I noticed in the last phase, a short, steep hill with sharp bends; then a mile or two of straight and a turning. At this point the other chap in the van stuffed my ears with cotton-wool and pulled a black bag over my head. Ivanovitch assured me that I need fear nothing.

Now we went down a long slope over a roughish road; and after it, just before we stopped, came an abrupt leap upwards which I took to be the drive into a house. I was carried out of the van and down some steep steps. I was then set free of bag, ear-plugs, cords and all, and found myself in a basement room or cellar, carpeted and fitted up with table and chairs. It had no windows, and was lit by a modern paraffin lamp.

Yegor Ivanovitch offered me a drink with the unmistakable neutrality of a policeman. His manners, perhaps, simulated cordiality more lightly than those of Scotland Yard. He seemed to consider drinking a ceremony which had its own rules, however unpleasant the business to follow. Of that I was glad, for I badly needed a moment's relaxation.

'And now,' he said, offering me a chair at the table, and taking one himself at the opposite side, 'let us have a talk. You have done me a great favour.'

I didn't much care for this surprising opening, or for my position on the wrong side of his temporary desk; so I smiled and said nothing.

'These "moths" you were collecting . . .' he went on. 'But it seems that everything else you told me last night was true?'

'Within reason,' I answered.

'Within reason, of course. It may interest you to know that I have made a careful study of English police methods?'

He had a habit, which laid a polite veneer over interrogation, of making a casual, plain statement and ending the sentence as if it were a question.

'I hope you have profited by them.'

'Profited? No. They cannot be adapted to our greater economic freedom. I was going to tell you only that I know your police never break the law.'

'Sometimes they must,' I answered, hoping that he would take me to have acted in an official capacity.

'Never! Nor your secret police either, such as they are. No, Mr Taine, you don't belong to *them*. I think you must be just a friend of Commander . . .' and he gave Pink's real name.

'No,' I said. 'A little more responsible than that.'

Score one for him. I was so anxious to make myself out a person of importance who would be missed at once that I had admitted Pink's identity.

He did not show the least awareness of his success.

'More responsible? One of his fascists then?'

'I'm damned if I was!'

He begged my pardon effusively. However well he knew us, he could not guess that to most Englishmen the word *fascist* was more comic than insulting.

'This anarchistic, individual patriotism is hard for me to understand,' he said. 'There are so many of you English who will act for your country without orders, and never care if you are disowned afterwards. Mr Taine, I am going to assume that you have no sort of official position?'

'If it suits you.'

'Now why should we fence? Let us be allies as during the war. Yes, in this I am sure I may consider us allies.'

'Better be careful you aren't shot when you get home,' I said.

'Shot? Why? I should not be shot if I made a mistake. I should be sent to work for my country wherever work was hard and unpleasant. Mr Taine, I have been watching that criminal Losch for some weeks.'

'Odd we never saw each other,' I remarked.

I couldn't get a single shot on the target. He just laughed.

'But I am telling you the truth!' he assured me. 'And because we never did meet, I know that you and the commander have hardly watched at all. Please try to be frank with me as I am with you.'

He offered me another drink which I refused, and then adjusted the lamp. It was vile to remember that there was a Dorset summer day outside.

'I am so sorry. I am afraid the light has been in your eyes,' he said. 'Mr Taine, I give you my word that I and my staff were sent to England to find those ticks and prevent them being used. My inquiries led me to suspect Losch, but I could not be sure – until the commander interrupted us last night. Please do not believe that we Russians have horns and hooves. We are men like you. We do not come out of police romances. We do not spread diseases.'

'It would be so awkward if you were caught,' I replied, remembering Roland's chief objection to believing a word of Pink's story.

'Of course,' he agreed. 'And there is another thing you must understand. The relations between our government and the new People's Democracies are not at all what you think. We cannot compel obedience. We can only advise and apply a tactful pressure. These Germans and Poles and Czechs – we have no more power over them than your own parliament over the legislatures of crown colonies. Were you ever in civil affairs in Germany?'

'No, thank God!'

'It is a pity. You would have realized our difficulties. We cannot make communists of the Germans, Mr Taine. We can only make soldiers. And you will never make of them your so-called democrats. You will only make soldiers. They have no sense of politics, no sense of anything but to impose their hysterical will. This' – he touched Pink's vasculum which was strapped to his waist – 'is their doing, not ours.'

'What about the Colorado beetle story?' I retorted. 'Don't tell me your propaganda people didn't think that one up!'

'I think it probable. What else could they do? Suppose I had not got on to the track of Losch in time, whom would you have blamed when you found out the cause of your dying cattle? For the sake of all who trust us to give them a world of freedom, we had to have a story ready. Colorado beetles!' – he laughed with a note of pity – 'an invention good enough for the masses as they are – but not, Mr Taine, for the masses as they will be.'

'What are you going to do with Losch?' I asked.

'I had a short interview with him last night after I left you. He is a party member and will obey. He will go to Russia in my care.'

That seemed to me a grim and entirely fitting journey for Losch. Lord help me, I was inclined to think quite kindly of Ivanovitch! The extreme daring and efficiency with which he and his little band of agents operated in a foreign country compelled admiration.

'You propose that I should go too?' I asked.

'Whenever you wish, Mr Taine, I shall be delighted to see that you are given a visa. But all I want now is your help. And I am sure I will get it. This matter, you see, is now cleared up. When I left Losch, the thorns were burning in his fireplace. This case of yours I have. And in a week or two there will be nothing in Tangier to worry either of us. This absurd, unauthorized weapon in what you call the cold war will be as if it had never existed.'

'The commander?'

'An ex-fascist, a paid jackal, a murderer and now a bandit,' he answered with a contemptuous hatred that boded ill for Pink. 'Would anyone in their senses believe him?'

'But he has been believed,' I said.

'No, Mr Taine, he has not; if he had, Losch would be in the hands of the police, or every contact of his watched day and night. No, no, I can avoid all unpleasantness if you are silent. And why should you not be? I am sure you do not wish to make trouble between allies.'

I replied cautiously that no one wished to make unnecessary trouble, and that if his Embassy were to explain the true position as he had explained it to me, any action taken would certainly be discreet and unofficial. We all knew the capacity of Germans for running wild.

'That is most friendly,' he said. 'I knew that I could count on you. But there are difficulties. My little party, with Losch, must leave the country. And then we must have time to handle Holberg ourselves. That means, I fear, that I must *ensure* your silence.'

'I tell you straight that if I'm not seen again and soon, Pink's story will be believed,' I said.

'Of course. That is obvious.' Yegor Ivanovitch replied. 'Besides, I have no right to detain you. It would not be ethical. No, but I am bound to insist that you keep silent for, say, a couple of weeks.'

'That's an impossible request. I won't.'

'I think you will. Excuse me a moment.'

He went out, holding the door open long enough for me to see that there were a couple of solid-looking toughs outside it, one of whom had been with him in the van. Ivanovitch must have been given his pick from the whole of his service, for every one of his men could pass as British in appearance and language.

That room was like a tomb. I could hear nothing whatever. The four whitewashed walls were round me, blank and unbroken by any object but a loudspeaker high up in a corner. I thought of knocking the lamp over, but there was nothing which would burn except the carpet and myself. I thought of hiding behind the door and laying out Yegor Ivanovitch when he returned. That didn't lead to anything constructive either. I lit a pipe and sat down, and tried to imagine some way by which my silence could be ensured without killing or keeping me.

Ivanovitch returned after about a quarter of an hour. The two men outside entered the room with him.

'You must now prepare yourself for a shock,' he said. 'But please remember that we Russians have most gentle and kindly hearts, and that you have nothing to be alarmed about. I want you to listen to that loudspeaker.'

He touched a switch beneath it. I couldn't for a moment make out the sound I heard; then it was clearly a child sobbing. I looked at the three men, puzzled. The child was sobbing in a rhythm very like George's; but still I could not understand.

Then Jerry's voice came through, as firmly as if he were in the room. He was playing the bold man for all his seven years were worth, and imitating the very tone in which I would comfort either of them when they were upset for no good reason.

'Don't *cry*!' he said. 'If Daddy sent the car for us, Daddy must be here.'

I gathered my feet under me and smashed the nearest Russian. It did me a bit of good to see him spitting blood, but the savagery was utterly futile. Yegor Ivanovitch had his pistol trained on me. He did not even look at his hurt man. The discipline in that team was absolute.

'If you make me kill you, they can never go back to their mother,' he reminded me. 'Sit down!'

I sat down.

'They locked the door,' George wept.

'I don't suppose they did *really*,' Jerry answered. 'Use your handkerchief!'

I was so proud of him. I would have sold my soul to the devil.

'Enough?' asked Ivanovitch.

'Enough.'

'I had better tell you what happened,' he said, 'so that you will know the explanations you must give. My assistants took your car and called for the children at the school, saying that you wanted them home for lunch. The mistress knew your car, of course. Why should she question it? A mad risk to take, yes – but I have had so little time for planning. Mr Taine, we are both very lucky. If you had not taken the road to Dorchester this morning, you would have been shot from the roadside between your house and the village. If I had not got your children, you would be shot now. But at last we can breathe. We have time. Time,' he repeated with a gasp of thankfulness.

'How much time do you need?' I asked.

'I told you. A week or two.'

'And if I do not say a word . . .?'

'If you and your wife do not say a word, if you can pretend that they have gone – oh, to their grandmother, for example – then they will be returned to you at the first possible opportunity. But do not be impatient. It may be difficult.'

'Why difficult?' I stormed.

'Because, Mr Taine, your children and Losch and ourselves will all, I hope, be out of the country tonight. We shall leave by private means, and I shall restore your children by private means. If you inform the police, you might make it quite impossible for me to return them at all. I cannot, you see, simply put them on a channel boat under the eyes of the world. I must be sure that no one but you is looking out for them or expecting them.'

I begged him to let me speak to the children, but he would not. He apologized for this cruelty – he frankly described it as cruelty – explaining that the children had seen in what direction and where they had been driven.

'In fairness to them,' he said, 'I cannot allow you to have the least idea where you are. If you knew, the temptation to appeal to the police would be irresistible. And now we must hurry, if you are to get back in time to warn your wife. You will persuade her not to be foolish as best you can. Everything else I have arranged for you.'

My mind was in a blank prison of helplessness. How I could get my boys back, how I could face Cecily – those two questions were swirling through my head like a fever dream. I wasn't thinking at all. I was simply exclaiming to myself.

Yet then, in that room, it wouldn't have helped me if I could have thought with the clarity of a chess-player. There was nothing I could force Yegor Ivanovitch to do except to kill me. That, it is true, would have badly upset his plans. Cecily, finding herself in the evening without children or husband, would have instantly got in touch with Roland, and the next day the police would be in action all over the country. But would the police succeed in finding this hideout? And, if they did, would they find it in time? Ivanovitch talked of leaving that very night.

'I shall take you back in the van as you came,' he said. 'I need hardly tell you that the registration number which you have seen is false. I shall then leave you with your car, not far from your own home. One of your tyres will be flat, and you will have to change the wheel. That will prevent you following us. And please do not have any fear for your brave boys. We are all fathers. And it is the first duty of a Russian citizen to care for the next generation.'

I submitted to the indignity of being trussed up again. Good Lord, they could have insulted me as they pleased – painted my nose blue or made me sign any confession they wished! I was in such a state that I would have welcomed it. To be humiliated was a sort of expiation for my folly. Never again will I despise those chaps who heap unnecessary dirt upon themselves at state trials.

All went as Ivanovitch had said it would. The drive was longer, and over a rougher road than that by which we had come. At last the van stopped. I was untied and pushed out. Simultaneously the man who had been driving my car to the rendezvous jumped in. The van roared away. My car was standing on the green verge of a country lane, pointing in the opposite direction to that in which the van had disappeared. It had a flat tyre, and the jack was already in position.

It was 3 p.m. I had less than half an hour to get home before Cecily set out to fetch the children from school. My captors had run it fine. If Cecily showed anxiety when she found the children gone, there was little we could do thereafter to hush up their disappearance.

I changed that wheel in record time, and drove straight up the lane to higher ground. In two minutes I was on the top of the downs, and saw below me a long village street which I recognized as Piddletrenthide. In ten more minutes I was at my door.

What happened between Cecily and myself is nobody's business but ours, and neither of us want to recall it. Had she been, from the start, eager and willing that I should work for Roland, we might perhaps have broken down in tears together over our joint folly. As it was, I was overwhelmed by guilt. There was I, well, alive, unhurt, without the children.

The telephone had been mended. I tore it out of her hands

when she insisted on calling the police. I drove it home to her that Yegor Ivanovitch could never take the risk of returning our boys if the police were on the lookout for them; any man seen with them, here or abroad, would be instantly arrested and his contacts and antecedents traced.

I tried to explain to her that, after all, Ivanovitch wouldn't want to be bothered with them more than necessary; that when he had destroyed all the evidence of those cursed ticks in Tangier, he wouldn't mind what story I told, and would have no need to hold any hostage for my good behaviour.

I came alive in my eagerness to persuade myself that what I said was true. It is odd that one can show more emotion in convincing oneself than another person. Up to then I had spoken with a dreary, artificial calmness, and called it self-control.

'Why should he ever return them?' she cried at me. 'What about the Greek children?'

'But what could I do?' I implored her.

'You came home without them.'

I moved away to pour myself a drink, to pick up the paper, to do I know not what in order to separate myself from my beloved. Meanwhile she prowled back and forth across the room, dead white, her eyes cold with torture and anger. When I said something – some worthless idiocy to try to restore an unrestorable normality – she shouted at me to leave her alone to think.

'Losch – was he at this house?' she asked.

'I don't know. I don't believe he was.'

'Why wasn't he? Oh, pull yourself together and *think*!'

That last word seemed to be forced from her by a super-human effort of throat and tongue, as if it were a muscular compulsion upon both of us.

'Because he couldn't just vanish,' I answered. 'Because he's a respected citizen of Bournemouth. Ivanovitch must have left him free to clean up his affairs, whether he liked it or not.'

'Why doesn't Losch go to the police? Does he expect any mercy when he gets to Russia?'

'He might,' I answered. 'More than here, at any rate. And Ivanovitch has a way with him.'

'Oh, you!' she cried. 'You can't think badly of anyone who offers you a drink. But Losch?'

'How *can* I know what he hopes? They may have offered him a laboratory beyond the Urals where he can't get into trouble. Something of that sort would be their game.'

'Would he be watched?'

'How can I know?' I repeated hopelessly. 'Perhaps. But Ivanovitch can't have men for everything. They may just fetch him when they are ready.'

'Get him first,' she said. 'You and Pink.'

I couldn't even judge her proposal on its merits. We were so limitlessly apart that nothing either of us said had meaning. I was determined not to compromise the children. I insisted that it was too great a risk.

'There isn't any risk that is too great,' she answered frantically.

I didn't agree, but her tone stung me at last into constructive thinking. It might well be that Yegor Ivanovitch had left one untidy end in all his quickly improvised planning; after all, it was only a little over twelve hours since Pink had made his disastrous appearance at my car.

Cecily perceived my change of mood – though I do not remember saying a word – and her eyes were fixed on me more kindly.

'Don't stay with me,' she said, 'and don't listen to me! But just remember Losch! When you are with Pink, you'll – oh, you'll see more clearly. I can't advise you.'

I wanted her to go away for the weekend – partly so that

she wouldn't be alone in the house, and partly so that I could communicate with her safely. She wouldn't hear of it. She couldn't bear the thought of the children coming home – unlikely though it was – and finding the door locked. She understood that she might be condemning herself to remain without news of any of us beyond, perhaps, a very guarded telephone call. Such patient courage is beyond me.

I changed out of my London suit, and took with me kit for a couple of nights. I looked longingly at my old army revolver, but I had no ammo for it, and I'd had enough of empty pistols. Then I drove down to the office and told my clerk that I was taking the children away for the weekend and might not be back till Tuesday.

I found a message on my desk that Dorchester police had telephoned. I called them back, in an intolerable mood of wild hope that they were going to report some suspicious circumstance which might lead straight to my boys, and of dread lest they had found out just enough to force my hand, and no more.

The reason for the call was plain routine. The inspector wanted to know if the person who had talked to a constable in Bournemouth at 2 a.m. had really been me.

'I didn't know you collected moths,' he remarked invitingly.

He was the same inspector who had been just too late to run me in the previous autumn. Ever since he had regarded me as a first-class subject for nods and winks and knowing conversation.

I couldn't pull myself together, and made some stammering reply to the effect that I'd caught butterflies ever since I was a boy. He thought, I am sure, that I was embarrassed at being detected in so infantile a hobby.

'What was it all about?' I asked him.

'Someone broke into a Dr Losch's house. Nothing

missing, though he did a power of damage in getting out. You ought to know of Losch if you collect moths.'

I nearly said I didn't, and then had a flash of inspiration.

'I did just meet him once,' I replied. 'He struck me as a nervous sort of chap.'

'What made you think so?' he asked at once.

'Oh, just an impression.'

'Well, you summed him up all right. He was burning something in his chimney early this morning, and now he has told Bournemouth police that he is so upset he has to go away for a week or two.'

'You seem to know a lot about the case,' I said.

'Oh, as soon as your name came up, I thought I might as well find out all I could, you see.'

'No,' I assured him, 'I wasn't pinching his spoons for the prime minister or anything. By the way, who was that officious ass who wanted to have me run in?'

'Just a journalist of some sort who has had rooms across the road from Losch for the last fortnight.'

I wanted to suggest to the inspector that Bournemouth police should check the antecedents of the journalist; but such a lead could only mean that I knew something and that I had not been on the scene by the merest accident. I was in no mood to be questioned. I had to tell the police all or nothing. And if I told them all – *you might make it impossible for me to return them* Ivanovitch had said.

I got to West Bay about six, and ran my car into a hotel garage where it wouldn't be seen by every casual passer-by. I was sure I had not been followed, but it was well to assume that I might at any time be in Ivanovitch's neighbourhood. I didn't know where in all Dorset he was, and had not the least clue.

The wind had been freshening all day. The headlands of Devon were a long black line in the west with black clouds above them; but the sun was out, and the even, white-capped seas racing across Lyme Bay looked more exhilarating than dangerous. *Olwen* was not in the little harbour nor in sight. I waited for half an hour, and then I saw a speck of white, part solid and part a moving fountain of spray, coming up from the west.

I watched Pink round the breakwater with beautiful ease, and heard him exchange hails with some official on the quayside. He claimed to be making a passage from the Exe to Portland and coming in for shelter. You couldn't have disbelieved him. He was clean-shaven and fresh and merry with the sea. His white sweater and shorts, when he peeled off his oilskins, were properly expensive and weather-beaten, and, I thought, in convenient contrast to the dark clothes known to have been worn by Dr Losch's burglar. He was the very picture of a simple, healthy naval officer on a holiday. It might be considered a little odd that *Olwen* and her owner belonged to no yacht club, but their respectability couldn't be questioned.

It was the top of the tide, and he took *Olwen* up through the lock-gates into the lagoon at the mouth of the Brit. I hailed him with a surprised Good-Lord-who'd-have-thought-to-see-you. He played up splendidly and shouted something about not having met since Alexandria. Then he paddled the pram over and fetched me, and I went down into that desolatingly neat cabin.

'You're back from London soon,' he said.

I couldn't bring myself to give him more than an unrevealing, brutal outline of the facts. It wasn't that I had any resentment against Pink. He was in trouble enough himself. My story, when I came to tell it, seemed such a shameful admission of inefficiency and defeat.

Pink was gentle as a mother. I didn't expect him to have that characteristic. Yet I shouldn't have been surprised, for

I well remember one of my company commanders who was an angel to his men but couldn't be trusted to obey an order without embroidering upon it some fancy of his own which could involve a whole division. Pink wouldn't let me blame myself at all. That, I suppose, was what Cecily hoped or foresaw, knowing that she herself could only throw me into worse distress.

'Any idea at all where they took you?' he asked, after he had made me repeat and expand my wretched report.

'No. We went up and down a considerable hill, and we never seemed to pass through a town. That looks like the north of the country.'

'You can make your mind easy on one score,' he said, 'they won't leave tonight. For one thing, we're in for a real blow, and for another your cloak-and-sickle man can't have had time to lay on the private transport he mentioned. After all, I know a bit about it – sea or air, whichever you like. And I tell you we've got at least twenty-four hours to play with. Look here, we'll get back into the harbour while the tide serves. We might want to go to sea in a hurry.'

He took *Olwen* through the lock gates, and anchored in the outer pool. Except for a little coaster tied up to the quay, we had the port to ourselves.

'Had anything to eat since breakfast?' he asked. 'No, I thought not. Well, we'll put that right first.'

He produced a cold pie and salad and a bottle of wine. *Olwen* unexpectedly possessed a refrigerator.

'When you know you're going to be alone, and fitting out to be alone,' said Pink, 'you can find room for a lot more comforts than usual.'

As soon as I felt a more useful member of society, he asked:

'What does your missus expect us to do with Losch?'

'God knows. Exchange him, perhaps.'

'Bad bargain from their point of view,' Pink said. 'The moment you had your boys back, you'd go straight to the police.'

'I don't think she had any definite plan,' I said. 'She just spotted a hole in their arrangements.'

'We might as well see if he can be got,' Pink suggested cheerfully, 'and open up the game a bit.'

I didn't much care for opening up the game without having the faintest notion how to win it, but I was too grateful to think hardly of Pink. He hadn't said a word of his own troubles and of the fate that awaited him when Yegor Ivanovitch supplied the Portuguese police with a name for their set of finger-prints.

'If we could get Losch down in this cabin, we could probably make him talk,' Pink went on. 'I don't know, old man, where you'd draw a line.'

'Nowhere – so long as you've got a heavy weight to sink what's left of him.'

'That's the spirit!' he said. 'Now here's another line of country. If I were copped, the police would want Losch to identify me. Now, if I gave myself up, would that delay the whole party?'

I couldn't see that it would. The identification parade could not take more than an hour or two. I was thinking so deeply and selfishly that for a moment the magnanimity of Pink's offer went clean over my head.

'Good Lord, Pink!' I exclaimed, 'if I thought it would do any good, I'd probably have handed you over already!'

'That's the spirit!' he said again.

He made himself comfortable on the settee, and poured out some brandy. It was the first drink I had tasted without the feeling that I had no right to enjoy it.

'How many men has this Ivanovitch got?' he asked.

'Well, everything he has done could be done with four and himself.'

'Four's a lot. He could spare a man to keep an eye on Losch, or he may be right there in the window himself on top of his typewriter. If he is, shall we just bust in and tear him apart?'

It was a pleasant thought, but my mind was running on ways and means of getting Losch away from all windows and possible watchers. Identification parade – I kept returning to some idea vaguely glimpsed in those words. At last I had it.

'I wonder if we would be caught if we telephoned Losch to come down to the police station and identify his burglar.'

'Why the devil should we be?' Pink exclaimed heartily. 'And we must take a chance somewhere.'

His enthusiasm put me off. Suppose Losch telephoned the police station to have the request confirmed? Suppose Ivanovitch or one of his men accompanied him? Suppose we were arrested while trying to kidnap him?

'Yes,' said Pink, 'and suppose Ivanovitch doesn't see why he should return Jerry and George, anyway, and brings 'em up to be bloody commissars!'

That clinched it. I doubted whether the plan could succeed, but, if it did succeed, we might have Losch to ourselves for a day or all eternity. Assuming he had settled up his affairs and paid off his servants, no one would ask after him. The police would take it that he had done as he said he would, and gone off for a holiday to restore his nerves. Ivanovitch would think he had bolted.

'I hope he doesn't know much about English police methods,' I said.

'Don't care if he does,' Pink answered. 'But I tell you – because I've listened to 'em and I know – that a German in his position is going to have nightmares about the British

Secret Service. Losch will think there's no limit to what they might do. God, he ought to see Roland calling a conference to decide whether it's safe to pass a traffic light!'

I went ashore and called Cecily, just to say that all was well, and the night too dirty for anything but regular cross-Channel services to run. Then Pink and I worked out a detailed plan for the morning, and turned in. I tried to keep my imagination away from the three beings who were most precious to me, but I doubt if I slept at all.

We were away in my car at six. An early start was essential, for if we weren't back by eleven we should have to stay in that very public little harbour till the evening. Pink, knowing me to be an ignorant landsman, impressed it on me strongly that we had to race against the tide. We had plenty of time so long as Losch was an early riser.

At half-past seven we were exploring Bournemouth. We didn't care for its central police station; there was no handy quiet spot in which to leave the car, and far too much traffic. So we decided to invite Losch to Poole. It was highly probable that Poole police would have picked up the supposed seaman who had broken into Losch's house, and unlikely that any cop who knew Losch by sight would be on duty at the station.

At half-past eight Pink went into a telephone box and dialled Losch's number.

'Dr Losch?'

'Speaking.'

' 'Ere's the doctor for you, sergeant,' he roared. 'And yer tea's getting cold.'

I swallowed and twice tried to speak, and then my nervousness passed.

'This is Poole Police Station, sir,' I said. 'Very sorry to call you so early in the morning, but we should be grateful if you could come down and identify a man.'

Losch seemed thoroughly flurried. Yes, yes, he'd be delighted to. No, no, the sooner, the better. I told him that unfortunately our cars were all out, but if he would take a taxi we would refund the fare.

'For how long will you require me?' he asked. 'I am expecting a caller.'

'Not for more than ten minutes, sir,' I answered, 'and then we will run you back.'

He hesitated a moment and agreed to come at once. I suppose he thought that no harm whatever could come to him if he visited a police station in a taxi chosen by himself.

I came out of the box soaked in sweat from collar to socks.

'For the Lord's sake tell me what he looks like,' I said to Pink, for I had only seen Losch with his back to a lit room.

'Oh, you can't mistake him. Medium all over. Medium fair. Medium tall. Medium solid. Fleshy mouth, and wears glasses. Looks like any other middle-class German.'

It wasn't much of a description, but, after all, it was unlikely that more than one person answering it would drive up to Poole police station in a taxi at nine in the morning. I went into the station and hung about at the entrance, explaining that I was waiting for my brother who wanted to report the loss of a watch before going down to his office. I stood there, sweat drying, and shivering with cold, though it wasn't cold at all. The wind had gone down, and blue sky was spreading from the West – a reminder that by nightfall both sea and air would be calm for travellers, and that I had only the rest of the day in which to find Ivanovitch and my children.

Losch drove up a little after nine. He was indeed a colourless, obstinate medium; but I had no doubt that he was my man, for he was more than mediumly nervous. I let him pay his taxi and come half-way up the steps of the station. The driver, thank heaven, didn't hang about.

I greeted Losch briskly, and carried him along with me down the steps. When we were out of earshot of the doorway, I introduced myself as Sergeant Rogers of the C.I.D., and began a stolid, long-winded apology for a change of plans. We had had great difficulty, I said, in collecting a few men with beards to line up with our suspect. Parkstone station had now rounded up half a dozen, and, as it was easier to take the prisoner over there than to transport all the other beards to Poole, I would, if he didn't mind, take him to Parkstone.

I kept pouring forth explanations, with the reasonable deference of an efficient policeman to a member of the public, until we turned two corners into a lane behind the station where I had parked my car. Pink was in the driving seat reading a newspaper, his recognizable nose turned away from the pavement.

I opened the door and allowed Losch to enter. Then I snapped:

'Constable, you are on duty!' as if to rebuke my driver for his sloppiness in not at once relinquishing his paper.

'Sorry, sergeant! Thought I'd found a winner for Ascot!'

Pink came to attention in his seat with a stiffness that kept his nose firmly out of sight of our passenger.

I don't think Losch was quite happy. One plain-clothes policeman might pass, but he must have expected the driver, at least, to be in uniform. As we threaded our way through the traffic, I kept talking cheerfully about the burglary – trying to reassure him by my exact knowledge of times and places – and told him about the fight our man had put up before he was arrested. I described a wholly imaginary boat that he lived on, and said casually that he appeared to be a gentleman and had come from Tangier.

That had Losch thoroughly worried.

'I don't think the man I saw could be described as a

gentleman, sergeant,' he said. 'I don't think you've got the right one.'

It was sticking out a mile that he didn't know whether he ought to recognize Pink or not. That was hopeful, for it meant he hadn't had any instructions before coming down to the police, and therefore that neither Ivanovitch nor any of his men were within easy reach.

I had him so worried that he didn't remark on the roundabout but just possible route to Parkstone which we were taking. When, however, Pink turned away down the main road to Dorchester and the west, Losch took notice.

'This is not the way to Parkstone,' he said sharply.

'Damn, I wasn't looking!' I exclaimed. 'Still dreaming of Ascot, constable?'

That was the signal for Pink to choose the nearest place where we could have a moment's privacy, even the open road if it were clear. He apologized, went on a hundred yards and turned into a narrow lane which led to a boatyard.

As soon as the car stopped, Pink and I jumped out and changed places. He plunged through the open door and took Losch by the throat before the man had time to yell. Then he crashed down beside him, and rammed an open Norwegian knife against Losch's ribs.

'Put your hands in your pockets, and keep 'em there,' he ordered. 'And stay in your corner or this goes in.'

The car lurched as I reversed out of the lane. I heard Losch give a stifled cry.

'I told you to keep in your corner,' said Pink. 'Goes in easy, doesn't it? Now, Losch, no bluff! We know quite well that if you're found dead it will be put down to your Russian friends, not us.'

'Who are you?' Losch asked.

'Police, my lad. But not the kind of police you thought. And we don't want an inquest any more than you do.'

Losch began to bluster.

'Come off it!' Pink ordered. 'You've burned up your cattle ticks, so we can't bring you to court. But we're quite happy to deport you – or bump you off if you prefer it.'

That was the end of the first act, which, Pink had insisted, was his sort of business; and indeed I was far more ready to trust him than myself. The mention of cattle ticks had reduced Losch to a medium jelly. It was now my turn to join in with an air of authority. I stopped the car, and turned round to address him.

'Dr Losch, you will understand that it is not convenient for the government to have any knowledge of your existence, so my orders are to deport you privately. If you come quietly, you will be landed on the coast of France and left to get in touch with your friends as best you can. If you do not come quietly, the port police' – the idea of port police at West Bay was laughable, but he didn't know where he was going – 'have orders to detain us all and afterwards to hand you over to me. In that case I shall have no alternative but to take you away and dispose secretly of your body. Is that clear?'

'Hypocrites! Blasted hypocrites!' Losch screamed. 'I knew. I always knew. And you had the impudence to talk of Hitler's atrocities!'

'Hands in your pockets,' Pink reminded him.

I drove now with a good deal more confidence. One likes to keep the speed under forty when one isn't quite sure what may happen on the back seat. In order to avoid Dorchester, I went through Weymouth, where a last squall of thundery rain was driving the holiday-makers off the front and tying up the traffic, and then out on to the Bridport road where at last I could race that falling tide to my satisfaction.

Between Bridport and West Bay, with the sky clear, Pink

saw a constable standing by his bicycle and taking off his wet cape.

'Stop, sir!' he said to me. 'There's our man!'

That was a typical bit of Pink's daring. I sweated at what might happen, but I stopped.

'What's the weather in West Bay, constable?' he asked mysteriously.

'Sea's going down fast, but no day for a swim yet,' the policeman answered, grinning.

'All laid on, eh? That's splendid!' said Pink.

I drove on before he had a chance to embroider further. His move was terrifying, but a beauty – for it was absolutely essential that Losch should give us no trouble on the quay-side.

He did not. We had him out of the car, into the pram and on board in two minutes. Then I drove my car to the hotel garage where I had left it the previous night, and came back to find the anchor dripping black mud over the bows, and mud instead of water shining beneath the quay walls, and Pink dancing with impatience.

It was only half-past ten, but the swell from the bay was dropping *Olwen* a foot nearer the bottom than she should have been in its silky and hardly perceptible troughs; they were perceptible enough to Pink, and his softly steaming language left no doubt of it, especially when someone on the quay called him a damned fool who oughtn't to be in charge of a boat. Once we touched, and the water around us was suddenly thick with mud. Then *Olwen* cleared the breakwater and pounded her bows into a genuine green sea, and Pink cursed more happily.

The powerful Diesel drummed softly as we rolled southwards. The long line of the Chesil Beach opened up behind us, a deadly, desert shore ending in the savage cliffs of Portland. *Olwen* wallowed as confidently as a cheerful porpoise, and Losch began to look a bit green. We took him out of the cabin into the fresh air of the well.

'It's probably a more comfortable crossing than you would have tonight, Dr Losch,' I said.

'About the same, I should think,' he answered.

That was so promising a reply that I made the mistake of instantly slamming in a direct question.

'Where were you starting from?'

He looked me up and down with a faintly impertinent curiosity. It was the first time since he was kidnapped that he had regarded me as if I were a human being like himself, and not a mysterious creature of unknown powers.

'I do not know.'

'What were your orders from Yegor Ivanovitch?'

'To stay at home.'

'Why didn't you escape?'

'Where to? To you? Thank you, I would prefer to obey.'

'You are a member of the communist party?'

'Of the German communist party,' he corrected me.

'But you take no part in political activities?'

If he had been an open communist, the Dorchester inspector would certainly have mentioned it.

'I do not.'

'Are there many agents like you?'

'You ought to know,' he replied insolently.

He was winning all along the line. He must have assumed at first that we had rounded up Yegor Ivanovitch and his whole crew. My questions had now shown him that we had not.

'From whom do you normally take your orders?'

'From my superiors in East Germany,' he answered emphatically.

Ivanovitch had evidently impressed on him that, whatever happened, he was to tell the truth on that point.

'It was they who told you to establish those cattle ticks in England?'

'I know nothing of any cattle ticks,' he said.

'This man at the wheel – didn't he get some out of your house the night before last?'

'This man at the wheel,' he replied with a growing lack of respect for me, 'remarked earlier that he could not bring me to court.'

So he was certain that the vasculum and its contents had been recovered. I tried another tack.

'Was it Yegor Ivanovitch whom you were expecting this morning?'

'It was.'

'He telephoned you? A trunk call?'

I cursed the fact that I had been a plain infantry officer with no experience of interrogation. Losch was my master, he had probably been through several really efficient interrogations in his life before. I was sure that Yegor Ivanovitch had called from somewhere in Dorset – and therefore on the Bournemouth Exchange – and that Losch could never have had any impression that it was a trunk call.

'What were your orders for tonight?' I asked.

'I might be able to tell you that,' he sneered, 'if you had sent for me to the police station an hour later than you did.'

'Oh, to hell with him!' said Pink, exasperated. 'Take the wheel, Roger, while I go and heat a few things on the galley!'

He seized Losch by the back of the collar, propelled him down the companion and through the cabin, then hurled him into the glory-hole in the bows and locked the door.

I would not like to say whether Pink, when it came to the point, would have been capable of carrying out his threat. As for me, if ever I wanted to torture anyone, it was

Losch – both for the crime he was ready to commit against my country, and the contempt with which he had regarded me, lounging, positively lounging, on his seat. Now that we had arrived at the decision, however, I found that the brute's flesh was sacred to me. I can't think of another word. My whole ethical training, my system of taboos and religion and chivalry, vague as most men's though they were, forbade torture even for the sake of my children. At the time I was ashamed of this weakness. I put the matter to Pink in quite another light.

'If we ever have to hand him over,' I said, 'he mustn't be marked. And I'm not sure that it's safe to drop him overboard till we know the police have not traced him.'

'Got to break him down somehow,' Pink insisted. 'What made him turn nasty?'

I answered that I supposed it was good communist morale in the face of obviously unskilled interrogation.

'I can deal with that communist morale,' said Pink, 'if only you can hang on to your own.'

He turned east. With the sea behind her, *Olwen's* motion eased. When Portland Bill lay on the beam and about four miles distant, I saw white water ahead and asked Pink whether the wind was getting up again.

'That,' said Pink, 'is Portland race. Now, don't be alarmed. This is all for Losch's benefit.'

Alarmed! I should have been in a complete panic if Pink had not looked so mischievously calm. The seas had no shape or regular movement at all. They charged each other, and the white-topped, green columns spouted into the air, as if the shock of wave against wave was unyielding as that of wave against cliff.

'My God!' I shouted. 'Will she do it?'

'Oh, she'll do all right,' Pink answered, 'so long as the

engine doesn't stop. I'm only playing about on the edge. If anyone has got his glasses on us, he's going to think I'm an escaped lunatic.'

He played about on the edge, as he called it – though I could see neither edge nor end myself – for twenty minutes.

'Have a look at Losch now,' he said.

I staggered through the main cabin, hanging on to the table, and opened the door of the glory-hole. It was a small forecastle, of about four feet by seven, set between the cabin and the chain locker, and occupying half the width of the ship. The outer side of the one bunk had been built up to hold light but bulky stores. On the floor were coils of rope, fenders, paint-pots and floats for moorings. The glory-hole may have smelt like home to a seaman, but to a landsman's nostrils it had that faint, sour stench of any poorly-ventilated compartment in the recesses of a ship.

Losch was sitting on a folded awning, with a paint-pot, no longer empty, between his knees.

'What *is* this?' he moaned. 'What *is* this?'

The bows rose and fell a good ten feet, and I laid my breakfast before him.

'Just a bit of a lop,' I replied. 'Where would you like to be landed in France?'

I thought his answer might give me a line on Yegor Ivanovitch's destination.

He glared at me and retched.

'Where you please.'

'All right,' I said. 'No hurry. There's another ten hours yet, and we can always cruise around a bit.'

I shut him up again and lurched back to Pink and the blessed showers of spray.

'Got you down too, has it?' he remarked. 'I was afraid of that.'

I yelled at him that I couldn't help it and didn't give a

damn. That was true. It had done me good to see Losch, even though my stomach didn't think so.

'Any luck with the communist morale?'

'Not yet.'

'We'll try a little cat-and-mouse act then. I've had enough of this myself.'

He took us out of the race – not, I think, without difficulty – and *Olwen*'s bows dipped and rose in the regular run of the ebb-tide from Portland to the Start. It seemed to me like release from purgatory. The wind had dropped entirely, and the sea was only a smooth swell.

I had another look at Losch. The paint-pot had upset, and he had made no attempt to pick it up or find another. He sat with his head in his hands, drawing deep breaths of relief.

'Is that all of it?' he asked, as if to a fellow-sufferer.

He was so overwhelmed by thankfulness that he seemed to have altogether forgotten that I had no reason to have pity on him.

'Oh, well,' I answered, 'with the wind against the tide, it comes and goes, you know.'

I returned to the well and reported that we had, at last, a certain moral superiority.

'Back we go, then, and bust him,' said Pink. 'Courage, Roger!'

He put *Olwen* in the race for the second time. A great, formless ghost of foam crashed on the turtle-deck forward, and streamed away. Then the stern and half the length of the ship lifted clear out of the water. I never heard the screw race. Pink was a superb seaman, quick in anticipation.

'Short-circuit somewhere,' he announced. 'Do you mind working the hand-pump a bit before you talk to Losch?'

I worked that beastly pump for a quarter of an hour and showered upon it, I swear, long-forgotten meals. I still didn't care. Even when the swoop of *Olwen* seemed to leave me suspended in mid-air, stomach and mind were determined to outlast Losch. Seasickness, yes – but none of that fearful listlessness and depression which go with it. I might have only been suffering from a bad tummy upset on land.

'Have another try at him now,' said Pink, 'before he goes unconscious on us.'

That glory-hole was a hell of movement. For Losch it was like a butter-churn, except that he was never actually upside down. He had slid off his folded awning on to the floor. It was no place to lie; but his self-respect was finished.

'You said there wouldn't be any more. You said there wouldn't be any more,' he accused me.

'One never knows,' I answered, and gave him the rest of what I had, though God knows where it came from.

That was the last straw.

'I am dying,' he moaned.

The sweat and tears burst from him as he tried helplessly to relieve his nausea.

'A better death than Yegor Ivanovitch would have given you,' I suggested grimly.

'No, no. I am of value. He said so.'

'Nonsense. You would have a gun at the back of your neck the moment you stepped into that black van.'

'The black van,' he wailed. 'Leave me alone. I know nothing of the black van. I've never seen it, I swear to you. It was to pick me up at the Haven Ferry.'

'When did Ivanovitch tell you that?'

'This morning on the telephone. Leave me alone, man! I don't know anything. I only met him the night before last. Leave me alone!'

I kept on questioning him while he grovelled in filth and begged for peace. He hadn't expected any caller at all; he had told me that merely as a precaution. Ivanovitch had telephoned him half an hour before I did, and ordered him to be at the Haven Ferry at eleven, where, on the far side, he was to get into a black, plain van. After that he was to accompany Ivanovitch abroad. He swore that he did not know how, nor from where. I was convinced that at last he was whimpering out the truth. Ivanovitch was not a man to give away unnecessary information.

'Got anything?' asked Pink on my return.

'Get us out of here and let me think.'

The fact that the black van was to be on the far side of Haven Ferry meant – as soon as we were peacefully rolling again in sane water – a great deal to me. Assuming that Yegor Ivanovitch didn't want his van to be seen at Losch's house or in Bournemouth, there were still dozens of possible rendezvous on the outskirts, from which the roads fanned out to all Dorset and Hampshire. The ferry, however, was the nearest way from Bournemouth into the Isle of Purbeck, and a very long and unnatural way of getting anywhere else. Thus there was a strong presumption that the house where my children were held was somewhere on the peninsula.

Now, as county agent for my firm, I knew all the roads of Dorset, and at once I asked myself whether the few scrappy details I had picked up on my journey in the van could fit Purbeck. They did. The steep hill with hairpin bends could have been on the road from Corfe to Kingston. The short, level run was then east or west of Kingston, and the rough road downhill either dropped to the sea near Worth or Worbarrow, or perhaps dipped into the vale behind Swanage.

It wasn't much to go on. I had limited the possible area to perhaps twenty square miles of country, but those miles were full of lonely farms and cottages. Then I had an inspiration. Why had they put cotton-wool in my ears? What was I not supposed to hear? The sea. The answer could only be the sea.

I put my argument to Pink, saying that the only flaw in it which I could spot was that the van must have gone through Wareham, and I was sure we hadn't passed a town.

'If you drove in from the north and went slap down the main street,' he answered, 'you wouldn't have noticed it. Now what about those oil lamps you mentioned? Any help there?'

So far as I remembered, the Isle of Purbeck was pretty well electrified, but certainly the cottages and farms which lay down by the sea at the end of cart-tracks had no electric light.

'It's a nearly sure bet,' I said. 'If we can get any sort of confirmation on the ground, I'll set Roland and all the police in Dorset on it.'

We decided not to put back to West Bay and pick up my car. For one thing, my grey saloon would be far too conspicuous in the enemy's country; for another, West Bay was too small a harbour to risk leaving Losch alone on board, however tight we tied him up. Any small boy or holiday-maker might climb on board *Olwen* in our absence.

The glass had been rising steadily since dawn, and the wireless prophesied an anti-cyclone with light easterly winds. Pink thought he could risk anchoring at Swanage. We would then explore inland on foot.

He turned up channel, cutting across the tip of the race, now comparatively innocuous as the time of slack water approached.

'Mackerel and bacon sound all right?' he asked. 'You take the wheel while I cook 'em. Keep her straight for St Alban's Head.'

He went below and routed out Losch with a roar that reminded me of hard-case American mates in the sea stories. He stripped him to his shirt and hurled his revolting outer garments overboard. Then he gave him two buckets and a scrubbing brush, and set him to cleaning out the glory-hole.

I began to feel faint stirrings of optimism. The sea had

turned a summer blue, and against it, ten miles to the east, St Alban's Head stood up like a vast, misty, yellow mountain. The smell of bacon from the galley was glorious to a stomach as empty as mine, and a pleasant accompaniment was the sound of Losch's scrubbing brush, measured by growls from Pink and once the whack of a rope's end and a yelp. I couldn't help feeling that my luck had touched bottom and was on its way up.

Losch wouldn't eat; he only wanted to sleep. So we moved the stores down from the bunk to the now spotless floor, and let him climb up. Then Pink and I did justice to the mackerel, and smoked and watched the grim Purbeck coast open up to port. I had never seen those grey cliffs from the sea before, and I said that they must have been terrifying in the old days of sail.

'Lord, no!' Pink replied. 'If a skipper had weathered Portland and St Alban's Head, there was nothing here to bother him. And in calm weather it's been a pretty busy coast in its time.'

That was true. The sheer face of the cliffs and the terraces and ledges beneath them were largely the work of quarrymen. From the inaccessible caves cut in the rock-face, like the holes and perches of a dovecot, blocks of Purbeck stone had been lowered into barges and taken by sea and river to build the cathedrals of southern England and London itself, long before there were roads which could bear such giant traffic.

'Good smuggling coast, too,' said Pink. 'Some of those ledges are like quays. On a calm day I'd take *Olwen* alongside and let you walk ashore.'

'If Yegor Ivanovitch is using someone like' – I was a bit embarrassed – 'well, the sort of thing you met at Tangier, could his skipper send a boat ashore at Seacombe or Winspit or any other of those ledges?'

'Of course he could, given a dark night and fair weather

and a hand in the dinghy whom he could trust. I'd rather use Poole. Only Poole – well, the quieter places are a bit tricky even for *Olwen*'s draught, and the port control has been tightened up recently. It's such a dam' obvious place for any sort of racket. But look here – if the job was urgent and there wasn't much sea running, I'd guarantee to take half a dozen chaps off any of those ledges' – he waved a hand at the forbidding and apparently sheer face of the cliffs – 'and pick up my dinghy and be off to sea in twenty minutes without a single bloody coastguard being any the wiser. And if he did see me and wonder what I was doing so close in, he couldn't read my name.'

When we rounded Peveril Point into Swanage Bay, Pink stopped the engine and fell upon the sleeping Losch. We tied up his hands and feet, and gagged him with a field-dressing strapped across his mouth by plenty of adhesive tape. We had to make a port, we told him, for repairs to the engine, and he could go to sleep again without fear. Then Pink put into Swanage, and, finding no safe anchorage for craft of *Olwen's* size, persuaded a local fisherman to let us tie up to his moorings.

We dressed ourselves from Pink's wardrobe to resemble a hearty pair of holiday-makers. I put on sun glasses, and Pink concealed the shape of his nose with a pad of lint and sticking-plaster. In Swanage we bought two knapsacks, and stuffed them to a proper bulkiness with loaves and sweaters. Neither of us could possibly be recognized at a distance, and that was all we wanted. The occupants of the house, whoever they were, were bound to be so used to summer traffic that they would pay little attention to hikers on the cliff paths.

All this took time, and it was four in the afternoon before we left Swanage. There were still five hours of daylight, however – enough, if my theory were correct, to identify the house or the black van or both.

We strode fast over the bleak uplands between the main road and the coast, stopping only to investigate scattered farms and cottages. Often their upper windows looked out upon a horizon of empty sea, but they were set back too far from and too high above the cliffs to hear the waves in the strong wind of the day before booming into the quarrymen's cuts and over the flat edges. I was sure that the sound which I was not allowed to hear had been the roar of the sea. It could be nothing else. Yegor Ivanovitch didn't seem to mind my hearing any conversation of his, and the house itself must have been too isolated for him to worry whether I heard neighbours' voices.

No house would really fit my guesswork; and those which might just be possible were so obviously innocent – desolate farms with their cows and dogs and dung-heaps, or farm cottages with the labourers' wives feeding their poultry or chasing their children out of the peas.

We struck a little inland and followed the road to Worth. There the pub had just opened. We sat down in the bar and ordered a couple of pints. As it was a Saturday evening, three or four quarrymen were quenching their thirst already, and a couple of obvious summer visitors were starting early on their gin.

The landlord seemed to be a cheerful and communicative soul, so I told him that a friend of mine was staying somewhere in the neighbourhood, but I didn't exactly know where. Had he seen a shabby old black van going through the village the day before, and down to the sea?

'Don't come down for lobsters, do 'e?'

'No,' I said, 'not that van.'

'Then there's only Mr Firpin's van, what sells vegetables,' said one of the quarrymen positively. ''E goes down to Mr Fallot regular.'

That wouldn't do either. It seemed to me to stand to

reason that the black van couldn't be a regular visitor to the village. Yegor Ivanovitch must have whistled it up on that desperate morning when he called in his agents and decided to flit.

This Mr Fallot, however, appeared to have a house on just the sort of site I wanted. I asked who he was.

'Come down for week-ends. Ah, and any time he can get off, I reckon,' answered the landlord. 'Big Birmingham jeweller he is, they tell me.'

'Does he have people to stay with him?'

'Not as you might say, stay. He 'as 'is friends, though.'

He gave me an intolerably vague description of the man and of a servant whom he sometimes, but not always, brought down with him, which might equally well have fitted Pink and myself.

'My friend might have sent his children down in a grey saloon,' I suggested.

'Big grey motor car, was it?' asked the quarryman.

I gave him the number.

'Couldn't tell 'ee,' he said, 'but I saw a big grey motor car down to Mr Fallot's this morning.'

'Sure it wasn't yesterday?'

''Course I'm sure it weren't yesterday.'

'Children in it?' I asked.

The quarryman didn't know, but one of the summer visitors took his pipe out of his mouth and remarked:

'There was one child in it. I saw the car go through the village.'

I remembered George's habit of always going to sleep curled up on the back seat during a long journey; he couldn't be seen.

The evidence was muddled, inexplicable, illogical, as any other attempt to make clear sense out of human activities, yet it was somehow promising. Pink and I finished our pints and went away over the fields to have a look at this Mr Fallot's house from the other side of the valley in which it lay.

The house had been built in the between-war years, when anyone who chose to foul the cliffs of England by fastening his suburban nest on them was perfectly free to do so. This one, however, must have been planned by a first-class architect; little could be seen but a belt of shrubs, and behind them a squat face of Purbeck stone which was as natural a part of its surroundings as any quarrymen's cutting. Indeed the house looked as if it had been built on the floor of a shallow quarry. That was hopeful. Underground rooms or cellars could easily be formed out of the old diggings.

From the end of the valley track, above which the house stood, a narrow gully led down to a ledge of rock. This was surrounded by a crescent of cliffs, about three hundred yards across the horns. The ledge, formed by the cutting away of all the overlying stone, fell in a series of low steps to the sea – the lowest of all being about on a level with the mean high-tide mark. Old iron rings, cemented into a roughly-squared slab and rotten with rust, showed that the place had once been a handy quay to those who knew how and when to use it.

So much we saw during a casual walk along the cliffs and a scramble out to the edge of a low promontory from which we could look into the crescent. To keep watch on Mr Fallot's house was far more difficult. Those Purbeck uplands, bordering the sea, were a bright green desert. The steep side of the valley opposite the house was smooth enough for a man to slide down two hundred feet without tearing his trousers. A few stunted trees and thorns crouched in the hollows, and on the slopes were sparse patches of gorse and bramble; but there was no real cover except the loose stone walls that bounded the fields – typical moorland fields, empty and windswept.

It took a good deal of innocent wandering and lying about in the sun to find the shelter we wanted – an old home-guard trench cut precariously on the edge of the cliff, from which there was a fine view, through friendly grass and thistle, of Fallot's drive and front door. Pink wanted to plunge straight into it, but, as a once skilled infantryman, I wasn't having any. The strongest position isn't much use if the enemy has watched you occupy it.

And so I wasted more precious time. We pretended to admire the evening light on the water, and lay around like ecstatic townsmen, and not once did we look at Fallot's house until we had gradually disappeared into dead ground and so into the trench.

The house leapt close in the field of Pink's magnificent glasses. There was nobody about. On the drive, which perfectly fitted my memory of a short, sharp slope, I could see the recent tracks of cars. A chimney was smoking. The place had no electricity nor telephone. It looked innocent and respectable, even charming.

After about twenty minutes a man and a boy came out of the front door and went to the garage. I sprang on to the parapet to get a better view, but the boy wasn't Jerry or George, and the man I had never seen before. He took a large grey car out of the garage. He then stood at the front door saying goodbye to his host, and him, too, I had never seen before. They made a happy group together. I turned to Pink, yelping curses and obscenities. We had wasted an hour and a half of daylight, since we were at Worth, keeping watch on an obviously inoffensive house.

'Come on, old son! Let's not miss a lift!' said Pink.

We raced down the slope and were standing on the valley track when the man and his son drove past. He willingly gave us a lift up the hill. They were so happy, those two, excited by the wind and sun of the day. I asked, hopelessly, if he had seen another grey car with children.

'Odd that you should ask that,' he replied. 'We certainly did, didn't we, Jo?'

'That poor little chap who was frightened,' said Jo.

He was only about nine himself, but a thoroughly fatherly small boy.

'When?' I snapped.

The father looked at me with surprise.

'When we were driving down yesterday. Just like a grown-up, I said what a naughty boy he was. And Jo explained that he wasn't naughty; he was frightened.'

'Where? For God's sake, where?'

This admirable chap stopped his car and turned to me.

'They were parked by the roadside near Kingston, and we passed them about midday or a little after. Two men and two boys in a grey car. I say, is there anything wrong?'

I pulled myself together. There was nothing to be gained by starting a vast deal of local excitement until I had a direction in which to lead it.

'I'm sorry,' I said. 'The fact is I'm a bit overwrought. A spot of trouble in the family. Would you mind running us up as far as Kingston?'

At Kingston we easily got on to the track of my car. It had been parked on a quiet bit of road outside the village between twelve and two the day before. What had happened was now clear. After dropping me at the house, the black van had returned to Kingston; and the children, when they arrived, had been transferred from car to van. Enquiries about a plain, black van led us only to Mr Firpin again.

We offered a drink to our kindly driver and ice-cream to his son. They had both been fascinated by all this mysterious asking of questions.

'Look here,' said the man, 'don't think I want to butt in or anything, but aren't you police?'

Before I could reply, Pink took his nose out of his pint, and whispered:

'Revenue.'

You couldn't have doubted him. His tough face, brown above and red below, where two day's sun and salt had whipped the skin long protected by his beard, could only have been that of a criminal or some adventurous officer of the state; and since he had never lost his naval eyes nor his general air of authority, criminal was out of the question.

'After smugglers?' whispered our friend, and his son's eyes glowed in the setting sun.

'And bigger than that,' Pink answered. 'Now, sir, I think you yourself could help us a bit.'

The man seemed somewhat startled.

'Fire away if you've anything to ask,' he said.

'When did you arrive at Mr Fallot's?'

'This morning about ten. We stayed last night here at Kingston.'

'He asked you to come today?'

'Well, not exactly. Any Saturday, he said, if I liked to bring the boy down to the sea and have some lunch. So I thought . . .'

'Did he look at all worried when you arrived?'

'No,' said the man doubtfully, 'not worried, really. Busy, perhaps. He didn't have his servant with him, and kept us waiting a long time before he opened the door. But then he was cordial as you could want. You don't think there's anything wrong with Fallot, surely?'

'Lord, no!' Pink lied. 'I just wondered if he would be the right sort of chap to help us. Might be useful with a house right on the sea. Have you known him long?'

'Off and on, since the war. I buy a bit of stuff from him,

you see. Theatrical jewellery and such-like. That's my business – masks, fancy dress, fireworks, comic tricks and high-class used clothing.'

'I always thought that was a Jewish trade,' said Pink.

'I am one,' replied our friend with delightful simplicity.

Pink's face pleased me, even among all my troubles. He had evidently liked this helpful and wholly English shopkeeper as much as I did, and just couldn't make him square with his favourite fascist theories. I felt certain that he was going to say *you don't look it*. He avoided that insult with an effort, but the next question rang too sharply.

'Do you buy watches from Fallot?'

'I do not,' the man answered. 'But if ever you wish to prove it, here is my business card!'

'Is Fallot a Jew?'

'Certainly not.'

'Does he sell watches?'

'Yes, naturally. Well, gentlemen,' he said rather sadly, 'I must be getting on.'

I tried to cover Pink's sudden change of manner by the sincerity of my thanks. There was no more I could do without giving away his offensive imitation of a suspicious revenue officer.

When the grey car had driven away, I fear I showed temper. Self-control was growing a bit thin, in any case, as the sun went down.

'Can it, Roger!' Pink said, unmoved. 'This is what I was after. Fallot may be in the same sort of jam that I was. Suppose he is smuggling in a big way, and suppose some old cloak-and-sickle got to know of it. Right! Then, Mr Fallot, you're going to run what we like when we like, as well as your bloody watches. Or else!'

I told Pink it was absurd conjecture, and demanded evidence.

'Firpin's van,' he answered. 'Look here – we've asked about the black van till we're hoarse. Nobody's seen it, and everybody's seen it. Now, I'm a chap who likes to accept what's under his nose without looking any farther. It's Firpin's van that you and your children travelled in. It must have had false registration plates when you saw it, but I'll bet it hadn't as soon as you were out of sight.'

I said wearily that I couldn't believe in my fellow Dorsetman, Firpin, Fruit and Vegetables, Deliveries Daily, handing over his precious old van to the Soviet Secret Police.

'It's a damn sight easier than believing Yegor Ivanovitch is God Almighty,' said Pink, 'and can whistle up ships and plain vans whenever he likes, and use 'em without any cover. I tell you he's got Firpin in his pocket. Why? Because Firpin has been running up and down to the sea and carrying whatever Fallot gave him under the vegetables.

'Lord, Roger, it's just like those communists! They blackmail two perfectly decent smugglers, and before the poor chaps have time to look round they find they've become proper criminals and are doing whatever they're told to do. Even so, I bet you anything, they don't know it's a political gang they are working for.'

Well, it was possible. Indeed, it was nearly certain that the black van was Firpin's. But was Firpin's chief or partner Fallot? If Pink was right and if his smugglers had to accept any yarn that was served up to them and didn't know in whose power they were, then any of those seemingly innocent cliff-top farmers were as likely as Fallot.

Pink had to agree, but stuck to his Birmingham jeweller. It was well known, he said, in Tangier that a man could soon retire on the proceeds of running watches and jewellery into England.

It was now half-past eight. We dared not waste time looking for Firpin – who, if he had any sense, would be providing himself with an alibi far away from home – and we could not call in the police. Help from them on any scale big enough to be effective was inconceivable; we had not the evidence to be convincing, and we had not the time. About all we could do was to get the local cop or coastguard down to Fallot's house – just enough to forewarn Ivano-vitch into final disposal of the children.

We had, at any rate, details sufficient to take action our-selves. Pink could not prophesy any hour for the arrival of whatever craft was coming. He himself would choose, he said, half tide or low tide, when the pattern of the ledges would be clear and a dinghy could be paddled in as easily as to a quay. Our objective was to delay the embarkation by frightening off the ship. I was to watch Fallot's house, and meanwhile, Pink would take *Olwen* to sea and watch the two or three miles of coast to eastward, where there were other possible houses, even lonelier than Fallot's, and other rock ledges accessible from the cliffs. We reckoned that we could upset the nice timing of their arrangements – merely, for example, by holdng any strange boat in the beam of *Olwen*'s Aldis lamp – and that by dawn we would have proof solid enough to bring in the police, and search and cordon the whole district.

Pink jumped on a bus and went down to Swanage. I struck across country in the last of the light, aiming for the side of the valley above Fallot's house. There was no one about. The quarrymen had gone home or to the pubs. The farmers were enjoying their Saturday night. There weren't even any campers along the cliffs, which were too bleak and windswept to be inviting.

First of all I fixed in my memory the exact point on the cliff path which was directly above two huge cavemouths cut by the quarrymen. Pink knew their position and thought he might even be able to pick them up in his night-glasses.

He was to keep one eye on the skyline above the caves for my flashes of light in case I wanted to signal to him.

When it was already deep dusk, I wriggled silently down over the turf slope until I was on the edge of the rough cutting in which Fallot's house had been built. Lying there – with my heels rather higher than my head, but firmly anchored – I looked down on the garden and the yard outside the back door. The front of the house was hidden from me, but I could see anyone who stepped away from it into the drive; and over my right shoulder I could watch between the headlands a black arc of sea. It was a perfect position – murderous if I had had a rifle and a legal right to use it. As it was, I had no weapon but Pink's Norwegian knife which he had insisted on leaving with me.

Fallot's house seemed abnormally quiet and dark for a place where the owner was at home and presumably enjoying whatever after-dinner relaxation he fancied. There wasn't a sound until, about eleven, somebody opened the back door and put the cat out. This innocent, domestic act gave me a moment of utter despair. There was I, fooling about on a dark hillside when my boys were in imminent danger.

The unknown lit a cigar and took a couple of turns round the garden and down to the gate, where he stood listening. There was nothing to listen to. The sea down on the ledge was so calm that at this distance its splashing was indistinguishable from the faint hiss of utter silence. Then he returned to the backyard and picked something up. I couldn't see what it was. There was haze high up in the atmosphere, and the night was black velvet.

He strolled down to the gate again, and out. I thought that he might be going down to the ledge to finish his cigar by the edge of the sea; but instead of following the little ravine he turned right and started to climb the cliff path. He was using a torch to see his way. As he came up to my level and passed within fifty yards of me, I watched the narrow pool of light travelling briskly along the ground.

The cliff path seemed an unnecessarily difficult route for an evening stroll, so I decided to follow him. Here at long last was a bit of a movement from Fallot's house which might repay investigation. I squirmed back from the awkward slope where I was lying, and then struck straight up the escarpment over the soundless turf. From the top I looked down on to the path, but there wasn't a glimmer of torch or cigar. I crept a little nearer to the cliff, and very cautiously – for although there was a stout wire fence to prevent one walking out into a hundred feet of space, the whole hillside was terraced with unexpected quarries.

After a bit, I heard a crackling of sticks well below me and to my left, and moved towards it. The unknown struck a match. I dropped to the ground and tried to resemble a large lump of darkness, for I was within thirty feet of him. Paper caught, sticks flared, and a fire of small logs began to waver and grow. The man then threw a handful of some chemical on the fire, and the flame and column of smoke turned reddish, yet not so red as to be wholly unlike an ordinary fire. Twice he fed it with his powder, then gathered the logs together to give a steady flame, and cleared off down the hill as if the devil was after him. I saw his face clearly in the glare; he was Fallot, the man I had watched saying good-bye – no doubt very thankfully – to our friend and his boy.

I had no doubt what that fire was for. The site of it was cleverly chosen – a flat platform set back into a second step of the cliffs. The fire couldn't be seen at all by the coastguards on St Alban's Head to the west, and was fairly sheltered from the east. And if it *were* seen, if even it were investigated, what was it but a summer camper's fire over which to grill his sausages? Very well that camper had made his fireplace, too, out of flat chippings of Purbeck stone, protected from the wind and with a primitive but satisfactory draught beneath. The stones were well blackened, showing that the beacon had frequently been lit.

I let the light of Fallot's torch disappear over the edge of the hill, and then I rushed down and kicked those logs out of the fireplace and stamped on them. I thought I saw two sudden and questioning flashes of light from the sea, but they were so quick and so far from the direction in which I had been looking that I could not be sure. A rough compass bearing showed them to have been west-south-west.

It was now my turn to do a bit of signalling. I trotted along the cliff path until I was above the two great caves, and found a long, low gorse bush which would prevent my light being seen from the south-west. Pink's position was east by south of the caves.

It was hard to decide what to send him. A single flash meant that he was to come in quietly and join me. Three flashes in quick succession would tell him to hang about in the offing as publicly as possible, with all lights lit. That, I reckoned, would certainly cause the strange craft to sheer off, but what might happen up at the house? If the party in Fallot's cellars – for I was now sure it was there my children were held – chose to escape in the black van or on foot, what on earth could I do to stop them? When we had decided that frightening-off was the game to play, I had not realized the awful blackness of the night. I could pass within twenty yards of my boys, and neither they nor I would know it.

I came to the conclusion that I needed Pink, and needed him quietly. I sent him single flashes. At the fourth my signal was acknowledged by a double speck of light impossible to notice unless one were staring out to sea along a compass bearing. In so vast an emptiness that tiny flick of humanity was comforting as fireplace and friend.

I made my way down to the ledge. As soon as I was past Fallot's house and off the turf, I had to feel twice with each foot before I dared set it down. Loose stone, old scraps of wire and slippery shale in the gully made vile going for a man who didn't want to be heard or show a light. The thought occurred to me – and I wish I'd paid more attention to it – that if I had to shift parcels of watches and jewellery I would choose an easier route. It must have taken me as long to reach the sea as for Pink to creep in two miles to his anchorage.

Close to the water there was a little more light, a spectral glimmer provided by the swirl and suck of the waves. I could distinguish the miniature dock, half natural and half split by Purbeck quarrymen, where Pink, if he could find it, intended to land. I walked out along its western arm, and then as far on as I could get over a spit of rock left bare by the falling tide.

I distrust the sea. Its romance in a sunlit, summer haven may pass; its reality, its own dark life among the recesses of a coast, is melancholy and alien. The steps of the ledges behind me, though Ivanovitch and his whole company might, for all I could discern, be squatting on them like gulls, were land and were friendly. But the sea which crept in out of the night and lifted the long strands of weed and plunged back with a smooth, gurgling surge of force was menacing and incalculable.

After a long wait among all these swirlings and reachings for me, I heard at last the plain, familiar sound of oars. It came from the west, the direction in which I did not want to show a light; so I returned to the solid footing of the ledge and tried to get within speaking distance. I was just going to risk a low call to Pink, when a voice from the sea muttered:

'*Verdammte Fallot!*'

I hoped that the unknown German was cursing Fallot because the beacon fire had gone out just when most needed.

The dinghy followed the gleam of lightly-broken water into a narrow passage that opened between the ledge and the western horn of the cliff. I came up close and, when I heard the sculls shipped and the crunch of the rope fenders, dropped into a handy crack among the limpets and sea anemones. I could just distinguish a tall figure in a white yachting cap who came ashore. He seemed to know where he was, and his footsteps padded away in the direction of the ravine and Fallot's house. He left behind him a seaman in charge of the boat.

When all was quiet again I went back to the little rock basin and showed a light low down on the water. I could only pray that Pink would approach from the east and land where he should. If he did, I thought it unlikely that the seaman, sitting two hundred yards away, alone in his dinghy among all those noises of bottomless drainpipes, would hear him.

I needn't have worried. When Pink came I didn't hear him myself. He was paddling the little pram with a single stern oar, and had muffled the gunwale over which it passed. There wasn't a creak or a splash as his head came to rest within a couple of feet of my own. He certainly knew his business a good deal better than the man who had landed from the dinghy.

I told him quickly what had happened. He agreed with me that the skipper of the craft lying somewhere in the outer darkness – whose engines he thought he had heard, but wasn't sure – had come in to get some sort of beacon going again, if it was only his own electric torch. Since his ship didn't dare to show any lights, he couldn't find his usual anchorage without help from shore; and more, said Pink, if he couldn't guide her in to where he wanted her, he would have a tough time finding her at all when he tried to return on board in the dinghy.

'What about you?' I asked. 'Where's *Olwen*?'

'Close in under the cliff,' he replied. 'Give us a clear sky, and you'd pretty near see her from here.'

I said that I had never noticed the beat of the Diesel, and he chuckled with satisfaction. It was his seamanship, I think, which gave him self-respect enough to carry him through personal loneliness and disaster. He explained that he had never used his engine once he was round the point, and had nicely calculated that what wind there was and the set of the ebb-tide would carry him close in to the ledge. He had unshackled his anchor and bent a cable on to it instead of the chain, and the two had gone down without a sound.

'Roger,' he said, 'it's unlikely, you know, that your friend in the yachting cap has more than one dinghy. And if he has, he'll have a high old time trying to lay his hands on it.'

'We'll give the general alarm if we pinch it,' I objected.

'Oh, I don't think so. The night is so bloody dark, and their plan has gone wrong, and nobody knows where anyone else is. Muddle 'em some more – that's the game! Skipper is on shore. Dinghy and hand vanish. No way of finding out what's happened without flashing enough lights to make even a coast guard put down his pipe and think! It might take 'em till dawn before they clear it all up. What was the chap in the dinghy doing when you left him?'

'Just sitting.'

'Well, you know how to get up close to him, so you'd better do the job. And I'll be handy in case of accidents.'

He took a cosh from under his sweater and handed it to me. It was just a steel bar wrapped round with tow.

'That's all I could make on board,' he said apologetically.

'Now, don't kill him. He's earning his living like the rest of us. Just a flick will do.'

Pink moored the pram to what remained of an iron ring, and followed me silently over the ledge. Given patience and slow movement, the job was easy. The man was still sitting in the dinghy with his head on a level with the rock. I didn't hit him quite hard enough, and he came round soon after we had worked the boat out into the open sea. Pink, however, quickly lashed his hands together with the painter, and threatened urgent death if he opened his mouth.

The seaman lay in the bottom of the dinghy, his head within easy reach of Pink and the cosh. I rowed for five minutes into the softly heaving blackness until Pink ordered me to ship the sculls and we glided up alongside the dim white bulk of *Olwen*.

On board Pink questioned the seaman, who understood a little German and a little English. He was some kind of refugee from the Baltic. Poor devil, he is on my conscience. He didn't deserve his end; yet I do not see what we could have done to prevent it. He admitted that the yacht had been smuggling, but insisted that he had only been on board a month, and was not in the confidence of the owner – to whom he gave some name that I forget. He couldn't, naturally enough, tell us exactly where his ship was. He reckoned she was something less than a mile off shore when he rowed the owner in. Her name was *Fiammetta* and her home port was Palermo, but she had been in the Channel for some time. She was reasonably fast and a good sea boat. There was one other hand beside himself, who acted as mate when required and could bring the ship in to her anchorage as soon as the skipper gave a light to steer on. There was no other dinghy.

We tied him up and put him in the glory-hole with Losch. Losch seemed to be resigned to his fate. His eyes, which were all he could move, followed our doings with contemptuous interest. He must have guessed that we were in serious trouble, and been thoroughly satisfied. He knew we meant him no immediate harm. Pink had given him food, drink and a cautious airing when he was clear of Swanage.

We rowed the dinghy back along the cliffs, and left it in a bit of a cave on the extreme east of the ledge, where it was highly improbable that the skipper would ever look. The ebb was going to leave it high and dry on the jagged boulders at the bottom; and if the flood didn't come in with a wind behind and batter it down to a keel and splintered planks, someone would be the better for a nameless lobster-boat which no owner would ever claim.

It was now after midnight. Fallot's house, which could have been seen from that far corner of the ledge, was dark. There was no more trace of man than when the Purbeck cliffs were made, and not a sound but the continual wash of the sea. We waited and waited. Once we saw two moving lights in the black sky, which might well have been up on the cliff near the spot where Fallot had built his fire. Once we heard, without a shadow of doubt, the distant beat of quiet engines.

It was an uneasy wait. We were alone on that ledge, and knew it. No one was looking for us; no one was concerned with us. Was that one hand on board cautiously bringing in the ship? Why was nothing happening? Yet there was no object in leaving the ledge for Fallot's dark house; we couldn't attempt to break into it, weaponless, against the opposition of Yegor Ivanovitch and his now considerable party. No, even Pink, to whom patience came hardly, admitted that all we could do was to wait until *Fiammetta*'s skipper returned to his dinghy; since he had only one, we must in the end hold the winning hand. It was the hardest wait of my life, for I knew that my children were in shouting distance of me, and yet might be lost by a shout.

I looked at my watch – an hour and a half since the skipper had landed. Long ago he should have signalled *Fiammetta* into her usual anchorage and started to ferry his passengers out to her. That was the moment we longed for – when men would be on the ledge who dared not show a light, men panic-stricken because the dinghy was not there, men scattering to find it. I felt pretty confident that in the confusion I could get my darlings into the pram and away. What was left behind I didn't care. Yegor Ivanovitch could be trusted to clear up the dead and the evidence.

At last the skipper returned, and alone. We heard him coming, and hid in that cleft, that chain of shallow pools, from which I had watched him land. He was in a hurry, stumbling and splashing carelessly across the ledge. He came to the cut where he had left his man and dinghy, and flashed a torch over the empty water. Then he called:

'Jan! Jan!'

I felt Pink's body stiffen beside me.

The skipper turned towards us, cursing in a low, furious voice, and Pink launched himself out of the pool like a leaping fish.

'Ritter!' he shouted.

Or was it a shout? To one listening on top of the cliff the noise might have been no more than a sudden and savage recoil of the sea.

He was at the man's throat before I could stop him or even clearly remember his deadly, justifiable hatred of Ritter. They splashed together, Pink uppermost, into the water of the narrow passage where the dinghy had been moored. The channel swallowed them, and returned to its sullen heaving and swirling. Then, at the short limit of vision, I saw two hands break the surface, one holding a pistol and the other clasped over it – such a nightmare as had seemed to me to be in keeping with that vile black water when I was alone upon the rock. I dived in, but the submarine battle had moved away. When I grabbed at a hand which touched my face, I felt only a long ribbon of cold weed.

There was a flurry at the lower end of the passage, and a wet back was outlined by froth and bubbles. When I swam to it, I found only a white yachting cap bobbing in the disturbed water which broke back from the rocks. Then they must have got their feet on solid bottom, for their heads and shoulders reared up with the fury of fighting seals, and someone flung the pistol to shore. The only voice I heard was Pink's – a coughing roar that shot the water out of his lungs. Again there was silence, and the sea pulsated between the confining rocks. Pink swam up the channel, and climbed, gasping, on to the ledge.

'Fixed the bastard,' he said.

I hoisted myself out behind him, and he whipped round with fingers outspread for my throat. When he saw who it was, he asked:

'You've been in too, damn you?'

I said I had done my best, but couldn't find either of them.

'Find? Find?' he cried hoarsely. 'No one will find him but the crabs. My God, and I suppose you'll blame me again now! I've killed Ritter, I tell you, and I don't care. If I've wrecked your plans, I don't care. I don't care, you hear me!'

He glared as if he were ready to jam me, too, in a crack of the rocks for the crabs to eat.

I quietened him as best I could. I was so thankful to see him, and I left no doubt of it. I would have preferred, it is true, that his personal feud with Ritter hadn't come up to complicate my own desperate quest; but mine was already so complicated that it was beyond telling whether Ritter's death in the darkness was for good or for disaster.

Pink clung to me – not, I mean, with his great arms, but

with that momentary spiritual agony of the soldier who has been let in for something beyond his powers and succeeded, and wishes to God that he were dead and covers it all with stupid laughter. And of course his loyal conscience was tortured. He knew very well that he had pulled a Pink on me at a critical moment.

This particular Pink, however, had acquired a Luger with ten shots in the magazine. That was itself a temptation to closer action, and closer action was necessary. Why had Ritter been going back alone? Had the transfer of passengers been given up? Or – probable and past bearing – had it been successfully accomplished somewhere else?

We went up to Fallot's house. To my surprise, there was now a light in a downstairs window. We crept round the blackness of the house wall, and looked in through the curtains. Fallot was thrown back in an armchair, his hands dangling, his eyes half-shut, in an attitude of infinite relief that told us more than all the mysteries of the night. Except for a lighted cigarette on an ash-tray and the whisky and soda at his side, he might have been dead. He was a pale, podgy man of fifty, and after putting up such active visitors I daresay he felt it.

The window was open at the bottom. I pushed it up, and Pink went through with the Luger pointed at that very fitting target.

Fallot thought at first, I believe, that these two savage, dripping arrivals were some of his own guests. No doubt he had seen as little of them as possible, and averted his shifty eyes from what he did see. He started a whole string of incoherent protests.

'I haven't left the house,' he cried. 'I haven't seen a soul. I won't talk. I swear to you that . . .' and then at last he seemed to realize that he had never seen either of us before. 'But who are you? Is one of you Losch?'

'What do you know of Losch?' I asked.

'Only that I heard them say . . . they wondered if I had warned him . . . they sent me to telephone . . .'

He went on squealing as if there could be no more hope in the next world than in this for crooked jewellers of Birmingham.

'There are two children here, Fallot?'

'There were. Yes. Belonging to one of them. I don't know which. I don't know anything. I had to do what I was told.'

'And how many men?'

'Five. But they're not here. Not here any longer.'

'Where are they? On board?'

He didn't want to admit that he had any knowledge of a ship. I drew the knife that Pink had given me.

'Yes. On board,' he screamed.

'Have they sailed?'

'Yes.'

I was mad with fury and disappointment, and I think I might have killed him then and there if Pink hadn't quickly interrupted:

'What? Sailed without Ritter?'

Fallot pretended he didn't know who Ritter was. Perhaps he did not. He whined that it was a long time since he had known any names. The skipper, he said, had gone back to his ship in the dinghy.

All this took less than three minutes. In the fourth minute Fallot was showing us his cellars. He didn't dare to deny their existence. He knew that death had come up from the sea into his room.

In his sleeping quarters at the back of the house was a large built-in wardrobe. He unlocked the door and pulled out the parquet flooring of the cupboard in a single block. Beneath it was an ordinary trap-door of deal.

Pink grabbed him by the collar so that his body was a

shield, and made him lift the trap and light the hanging lamp beneath it. We saw a steep, narrow flight of a dozen steps leading down to a roughly-squared chamber. Three sides were of natural rock; the fourth side of solid stone walling in which were doors.

We leapt through those doors one after another, Pink leading with Fallot in his left hand and Ritter's Luger in his right. There were three rooms, and they were empty. One was that in which I had been confined; it must have been Fallot's office for the interviewing of very private guests. The next was a cellar or warehouse, and had a safe in it. The third had not long been vacated. It was foul with cigarette smoke. Dirty plates, empty bottles and full ash-trays stood on a table of packing-cases. The room had been hastily furnished with deck-chairs, plain kitchen chairs and two camp beds. I made a quick search, for Jerry could be trusted to leave something behind him wherever he stayed. I found his tie. He had been amusing himself by weaving it in and out of the laces of the canvas bed.

'Where's the way out, Fallot?' Pink ordered, 'Jump to it, and remember that you're going in front of me!'

That was just what Fallot did remember, and he didn't like it at all. He tried to persuade us that of course there was no way out but that through which we had come. In the warehouse, however, was a locked door like that of a cupboard. I burst it open. Within were cold, damp and silence.

Fallot insisted that the space was only an old quarry chamber. I twisted his arm till something jumped out of its socket. I – well, I do not look back on that night with any pride. But I think their mother, gentle though she is, would have done much as I if had been given to her the strength and training.

With Fallot's limb revoltingly loose, we got a civil answer to questions. He told us that the quarry workings came out on the cliff face, some fifty feet above the sea. Immediately below the opening were two and a half fathoms of water at low tide. I gathered – for he was not always coherent – that there was an emplacement for a winch at the mouth of the quarry, and that he had received small consignments without ever knowing the name of the ship which brought them, or seeing more than vague movement on a deck below.

How did he know, Pink asked, that all the party was on board? He didn't, he screamed. That was the trouble; some of them might still be waiting at the mouth. It would take time to lower one man after another, and the two children.

Why wasn't he there? They didn't want him. They had worked it all out. They'd seen the place. All he had to do was to wind up the cable when they had all gone, and put the winch back, before daylight, where it could not be noticed from the sea.

Pink wouldn't give up the Luger, so he went first – behind Fallot, that is. The passage at first was roomy, at least eight feet across and as much high. It had evidently been cut out long ago without any purpose beyond the extraction of Purbeck stone or marble. It sloped a little upwards, and my compass showed the main gallery to be more or less parallel to the ledge, and bearing west.

Then we came to a narrow and very rough cutting, the floor steep and uneven and strewn with chips. This must have been made in the great eighteenth century days of smuggling to connect together two systems of quarries, and to give access from the sea to whatever building had then been on the site of Fallot's house.

After a minute or two of this dismal corridor, which wasn't much larger than a coffin set on end, we came up into a well-cut gallery, and then into the main level of the second system. My torch showed a space like the crypt of a considerable church, its roof supported by pillars of piled stone. We were under the small headland which formed the western horn of the crescent around the ledge. Fallot led us out by another gallery which sloped very slightly towards the sea. We were following the track along which the blocks of stone had been moved by levers and rollers to the face of the cliff, whence they could be lowered into the waiting barge.

We had a fair idea of what the end of the gallery would be – a mouth like those of the two caves above which I had signalled to Pink, but smaller, less conspicuous from the sea, and certainly no place for any sort of struggle.

As we approached the sea, the cleaner, warmer air was very welcome, and we shivered less in our wet clothes. They were a nuisance, those clothes. We couldn't move quietly. Every step was a loud squelch.

From the darkness ahead of us someone called sharply:
'Who is that?'
'Me! Fallot!' he answered, quickly prompted by Pink.
'Who is with you?'

Pink put on an imitation of Ritter's harsh voice. Booming out of the depths of the quarry, it was convincing enough.

'Ritter! My man has gone off with the dinghy.'

If it had not been for the challenge, I should never have noticed that we were nearing the end of the gallery. It showed only as a square of blackness defined against the other denser blackness. We were allowed to advance a few more steps, and then the figure at the entrance turned his torch on us.

We were at the limit of the beam and in single file close to the wall, so he couldn't see much. I reached an arm over Pink and Fallot, and blinded him with our own light. He was Yegor Ivanovitch, standing erect in the middle of the opening. I was already nearly certain of it from his voice.

'Kill him if you can,' I whispered quickly to Pink.

Pink fired and missed. I ought to have taken Fallot off his hands first, but there was no time for concerted action. At the shot both Ivanovitch and I snapped off our lights. The position was not healthy. We had no sort of cover, whereas Ivanovitch could jump in and out of the quarry mouth as he liked.

He was still doubtful what to make of us.

'Don't be a fool, Ritter,' he shouted. 'This is I, Yegor Ivanovitch. Fallot, who is with you?' he asked again.

I applied a little too much pressure to the arm, and Fallot screamed:

'Ritter, Ritter, Ritter!'

That terrified shriek was the end of all possible bluff.

'Shine a light on your faces and come out,' ordered Ivanovitch. 'If you don't, I fire.'

We dropped flat alongside the wall of the gallery. The shot ricocheted off the floor and went howling into the depths. I reckoned that Ivanovitch was using some light weapon like a .32. That was all to the good. If he had had a tommy gun or machine-pistol, he could have squirted bursts into the tunnel and been fairly sure of bagging us with direct hit or ricochet.

As we dropped, Fallot broke away and dashed down the passage, shouting his identity. Ivanovitch shot him dead as soon as he reached the mouth. Personally I should have preferred to hear what Fallot had to report; but Ivanovitch was taking no risks, and, I expect, had been itching to bump off his very shaky ally for the last twenty-four hours.

'I shall not leave you behind, Ritter,' he threatened. 'Come out, or I'll get help and fetch you out.'

The red stab of the pistol had come from the right of the cave-mouth. I whispered to Pink that I was going to crawl along the angle of floor and wall, and that he should keep his covering fire high. Ivanovitch could not know that there were two of us, and, if Pink could stop him showing his head or a light, there might be a chance of getting a knife into him before he ever did know.

I silently took off my shoes and coat and trousers, so that I could move unencumbered by drippings. That left a light gap between the dark of sweater and socks, but I comforted myself with the thought that it wasn't much lighter than Purbeck stone. I had about fifty feet cover, and I told Pink that I was going to do it mighty slow.

Pink gave me a couple of minutes and then fired two rounds. Ivanovitch replied at the flash, and I saw more or less where he was – behind a black something at the quarry mouth. I crept on until I reached it. There cannot have been more than three feet between myself and him, but the three feet were of solid stone.

My eyes, after the absolute darkness of the quarry, were more at ease on the edge of the outer world. The night, also, may have grown a bit lighter. I think it had. I could see the rock platform beyond the entrance to the gallery, and the winch and Fallot's body. The block of hewn stone between me and Ivanovitch stretched diagonally across the mouth, and was about the size of a single wardrobe lying on its side. If he chose to lean over it, he couldn't avoid seeing me; if he didn't, I had a chance of working round the end.

I followed along the inner side of the stone, inch by inch. Pink at this moment was inspired to fire a beauty which clipped the top of the block and must have encouraged Ivanovitch to keep his head down. I got my shoulders past the end of the barrier and out into the open, and then came to a full stop. Instead of the clean-cut stone beneath me, I felt rough grass and chippings. I could crawl no further without making a whole variety of little noises, and I hadn't a hope of reaching Yegor Ivanovitch over the top of the block.

The terrace or platform at the mouth of the gallery ran

out for some ten feet. I could see the two lines hanging down from the winch into space. Fallot's body lay crouched on its side in an unnatural position that a touch would disturb. I stretched out my left hand and pulled his boot. The body collapsed, and I made another foot under cover of the noise. Yegor Ivanovitch paid no attention.

Both Fallot's boots were now within my reach. Indeed, they blocked my view and obtruded themselves upon my consciousness. I was peremptorily reminded of a detestable occasion in the war when a pair of apparently dead boots in front of me began to drum upon the ground.

It was safe to assume that Ivanovitch had done a bit of execution before – for all I know, his branch of the Russian police may have to do a two weeks' course of it for promotion – yet he couldn't be wholly sure that Fallot was stone dead. True, he had fired at a yard's range, but the man had been in movement and the bullet was light.

I twitched the two boots in a gruesome imitation of Fallot's last expiring kicks. Ivanovitch hissed some curse under his breath, and made no move. He thought he knew what it was. I had not misjudged him.

Fallot's kicks gave me the last couple of feet that I dared take. I could now jump clear into the open round the end of the stone; but then to turn behind it and get at Ivanovitch was asking for trouble. It was a risk that I should have possibly have taken in war. Now, however, with the certainty that my children would be lost for ever to Cecily if I failed, I wanted something better.

Pink fired another shot for luck. After that the silence was complete. My back felt very naked. To see it, Ivanovitch had only to move to what I may call the neutral corner of the stone. I tried to convince myself that he wouldn't, for he must surely think that if he stood full in the mouth of the gallery, he would be outlined against the night sky behind. In fact, the night was too dark for any clear outlining, but that he could not know.

I decided to have a go at Fallot's boots again; if Yegor Ivanovitch's nerves weren't any better than my own, the delicate, intolerable sound might exasperate him into coming within reach. I was right. He could stand the twitching no longer. Perhaps he never took that two weeks' course after all. He crawled on hands and knees along his side of the block, and reached forth a hand to draw Fallot into cover, where he could deal with him.

As soon as his head was fairly out, I gave him Pink's knife between the shoulder blades. It wasn't quite enough. I am now ashamed that I was glad it wasn't enough. I turned him over and allowed him to see who I was, and to watch the steel as I drove it into his throat.

I shouted to Pink to come up, and crawled to the edge of the cliff. It overhung the sea. Almost directly below me was the dark arrow of *Fiammetta*'s bows. She was held by two stern anchors. A bosun's chair was just over the edge of the platform, ready for Ivanovitch. The line passed round the drum of the winch and down to the deck, so that he had only to step into the chair to be lowered. There was no sign of the children, and not a hope of getting down to the ship. In an access of fury I wrenched Ivanovitch's pistol out of his hand, and gave his body a heave and dropped it on two men who were standing by the lower end of the line. Unfortunately they looked up and saw it coming. The body landed on the forecastle hatch, and smashed it in.

This savagery did not pay. *Fiammetta* went astern, and Ritter's mate could be heard shouting orders to his passengers. There was an angry argument, dominated and finished by a voice which commanded the mate to get out of there and leave the traitor Ritter behind.

'Quick!' Pink exclaimed. 'Quick – for God's sake!'

I slipped on my shoes and grabbed my clothes. We dashed back up the gallery and into the main workings, where we had a horrible minute trying to find the right way out. Then we stumbled through the narrow connecting shaft, out into the lower quarry and so to Fallot's house. It took nearly a quarter of an hour.

Pink panted that we shouldn't lose hope, that Ritter's mate wasn't going to leave his anchors behind, that he couldn't be at both wheel and capstan himself, that his passengers were sure to make a mess of the tricky moorings; and he would idle as much as he dared in the hope of hearing a hail from the missing dinghy at the last minute.

We raced through the house and down the ravine to the ledge. Pink hurled the pram through the water, manhandled her into the well and on deck, buoyed and slipped his cable; and in twenty-five minutes from the time we left the quarry mouth *Olwen* was sliding through the calm sea on the improbable quest of intercepting *Fiammetta* somewhere to the south.

Pink, however, refused to call it improbable. If *Fiammetta* was bound down channel, her course was known, for she had to go south in order to pass clear of Portland and the race; if up channel, he reckoned that she would still hold a southerly course to reach the safety of the three-mile limit before turning east.

'He'll show his lights some time,' Pink insisted – though I could tell by his voice that it was more a hope than a sure opinion. 'Why shouldn't he? He's clear of the land, and he's no reason to expect anything on his tail. Damn it – he isn't Ritter! He'll be fussing over his charts in the wheelhouse, and he'll have to see to read 'em.'

He kept on mumbling to himself and peering into the utter blackness. *Olwen* was showing no lights at all.

Fiammetta, as our captured seaman had told us, came over

from Le Havre, but there was no ground for assuming she would return there. She might be bound for any port in Belgium or France where there was a strong communist organization capable of receiving Yegor Ivanovitch's special mission, and speeding it on its way to the east. And I think they all would have reached those friendly hands – minus Ivanovitch, that is – if a streak of complex illumination had not come tearing up Channel from Portland on His Majesty's business. She crossed our bows a mile or two ahead, and Pink muttered that if *Fiammetta* wasn't showing her navigation lights, that cruiser would have put the fear of God into the poor bastard at the wheel.

It did. On the starboard bow, at a distance I wouldn't attempt to estimate, we saw the red and white of a small craft. Both Pink and I were sure that only darkness had been there before the passage of the cruiser; so the presumption that these were *Fiammetta*'s lights was strong.

'Hell!' said Pink. 'Stern chase! And that man in the glory-hole told me she could do sixteen knots.'

'And *Olwen*?'

'About eleven. But *Fiammetta* won't do more if she hasn't got to, Roger. She can't have too much fuel, and her present course looks like Ushant.'

We sped steadily on over the quiet sea, and the limit of our world was the white water creaming away from the bows. I listened to the heartening beat of the Diesel, and prayed that it would not stop. The lights came nearer and nearer, and after half an hour we had them on the beam and, as it seemed to me, close to – though Pink said it was all of a mile.

'Now get this clear, Roger,' he warned me. 'If the hand in command of *Fiammetta* spots that we're after him, it's the last we'll ever see of her. I can't ram her because your children are below, and we mightn't get them out in time.

The only mortal way I see of stopping her is to board her. Take the wheel while I interview our friend below.'

Pink came back in a few minutes with full details of *Fiammetta*'s plan. He could get anything he wanted out of a fellow seaman. When he had water all round him he was a far simpler and more gallant character – nearer to his true self – than the erratic, disappointed creature of the land.

Fiammetta was built as a pleasure cruiser. She had an all-enclosed wheelhouse amidships, with the saloon and galley forward, and the owner's cabin and bathroom aft. There was a roomy forecastle with two bunks in it, which was entered through the forehatch which Ivanovitch's body had splintered.

'Could be worse,' said Pink, 'but it's like trying to board a bloody greenhouse. How much ammo have we got?'

'Five in the Luger, and four in Ivanovitch's popgun.'

'What is it?'

'Eight millimetre, I think.'

'It's mine,' said Pink, grabbing it. 'And I've got a spare magazine. More than you deserve, my lad, after pinching my gun that night in Bournemouth!'

Then he wanted to know what sort of a shot I was with a pistol. I could tell him honestly that at close range house-to-house stuff I used to be pretty efficient.

'If they take a look at you,' he said, 'they won't wait for you to use a gun at all.'

I hadn't considered my appearance. I had washed my hands overboard when we rowed out to *Olwen* in the pram, but that was all.

'Your face is as black as a nigger's,' Pink told me, 'but it's going to show nice and crimson when there's some light. Now, what I'm going to do is this: I'm going straight for them, and I shall blind the helmsman with the Aldis lamp. That's your moment – and you won't have more than five seconds before they're into us or past us. You'd better take my gun because we have enough ammo for it, and you may have to shoot away the glass before you can bag the helmsman. What will happen then, I don't know. But I'll try to tie the two ships up without doing too much damage. Objective is to take the wheelhouse and keep anybody below from coming up top. We ought to get two of them before they start shooting, and then it's only three against two. O.K.? And now lash the sculls into that pram!'

Fiammetta was now on the starboard quarter, and her green was at last visible as well as the red. Pink closed and closed, and for an interminable time we didn't seem to be able to force ourselves far enough ahead of her. At last he ordered me to lie down on the deck and get ready. *Olwen* heeled over in a tight semi-circle and we foamed towards the lights. Pink switched on the Aldis lamp, and I saw *Fiametta* racing towards us not more than two hundred yards away.

What happened then was all so quick that I have little idea of the sequence. I remember *Fiammetta* altering course to starboard, and Pink going to port. I smashed the glass of the wheelhouse and saw the helmsman raise his hands to his eyes. Then, or before, Pink roared, and there was a crash that nearly flung me overboard. I concentrated on my part of the job, shot the helmsman dead, and changed the magazine.

'Board, you . . .!' yelled Pink.

It was nearly too late. *Fiammetta* had cut right into our bows, and *Olwen* was down by the head and seemed to be slipping off into the sea. Pink leapt over me and jumped for *Fiammetta*'s fore deck. I followed him and missed my footing, but got a good half of me on board. By the time I had picked myself up, Pink's assault on the wheelhouse had failed.

The lights were on in the saloon, and illuminating the

wheelhouse from below. The four men had tumbled up in a hurry, and slammed the door which Pink was rushing. He dropped to the deck just in time to avoid a regular curtain of fire. I fell back on sound infantry tactics and took cover behind the fore hatch and Ivanovitch's body, which no one had bothered to clear away. Maybe it wouldn't move in one piece; maybe they had been arguing whether the State would approve of them chucking it overboard. The party in the wheelhouse put a few more shots into Ivanovitch, but they were lit up and I was not, and I got two of them. The third made a dash for the door, and Pink slugged him with his iron bar as he dived out. Number Four dropped into the saloon to put out those murderous lights, and stayed there. That looked very nasty for the moment, since anyone who entered the wheelhouse or tried to winkle him out was at his mercy. He had forgotten, however, the two forward ports of the saloon. Once those were smashed in, he had to watch them as well as the wheelhouse. And so at last we had the ship to ourselves.

The owner's cabin was locked. Yegor Ivanovitch, like a good civil servant, had reserved the best accommodation for himself and his personal affairs. We broke down the door. There on the bed were my two boys, asleep and lightly drugged. I thanked God for it. None of that horrible work nor the appearance of their father need ever remain in their memory.

On the table was the vasculum. Pink examined the contents at much greater length than was necessary. He could, as I've said before, be tactful as a woman in the face of another man's extreme emotion.

'Shall we take them to *Olwen*?' I asked him.

'Well, Roger, you certainly go all out for the business in hand,' he said. 'There ain't been no *Olwen* for the last ten minutes.'

'And Losch and that seaman?'

'Pretty clean sweep, isn't it?'

His fingers were playing drum-taps on the lid of the vasculum in the most exasperating manner. I took stock of myself. I had to admit that my violent trembling wasn't due to cold, as I had thought. I asked Pink if Ritter would have whisky on board.

'A vat, if I know him,' Pink answered.

I said I would look for it. I didn't want Pink to go through that wheelhouse and saloon again till he had to. My own share in that mess was justified. I hadn't a doubt of it. But Pink – I could see that, for the moment, he might find it difficult to call up a clear-cut motive; they were too many and too obscure. He had served himself, but even for him – especially for him, as I now knew him – that was no excuse for piracy and murder. He had served his country, but his country had not asked for his devotion and did not want it. He had served his friend, but it was he himself who had landed that friend in disaster and violence. As I picked my way towards the whisky, I swore that I would allow Roland no rest until Pink had been given back a right to be of use, free of fear and free of disgrace.

When I had the bottle – and another for emergencies – I removed the four corpses from the wheelhouse down to the saloon, and shut the door on them. Then we had a stiff drink apiece, and I tried to say how sorry I was for the loss of *Olwen*.

'Let her go,' Pink replied bitterly. 'I don't know if you'll understand, Roger, but I hated her. Or not her, you see, but that cabin. Week after week. Alone in it.'

Fiammetta rose to a bit of a swell, perhaps the last of the wash of some great liner far away in the darkness, and we heard the water rush and gurgle in the bilge.

'She'll do for a while,' said Pink in answer to my alarmed

look of enquiry. 'There's not too much damage. I think we could get her into port if we really set ourselves to it.'

He sounded confident, and *Fiammetta*'s engines were ticking over smoothly in neutral. I was becoming unpleasantly conscious, however, that my two boys and Pink and I were a long way from land with no boat.

'I suppose we wouldn't be in any serious trouble with the law if we brought her in, thanks to that' – he tapped the vasculum in which those much-travelled ticks were still lively – 'but, by God, it isn't fair to stick the police and politicians with a floating morgue like *Fiammetta,* if we can get rid of her. What do you think, eh? You're always yapping about the best service being no use without tact.'

I asked him what on earth he proposed. I wasn't going to push my two children ashore on life-belts. He answered that it had occurred to him that we might find ourselves – if we found ourselves alive at all – with no *Olwen* and a badly battered *Fiammetta*.

'And that, my lad, is why I didn't secure the pram,' he added with the proper pride that his foreknowledge of the sea always called out of him, 'and why I told you to lash the sculls in her.'

'We'll never find it,' I protested.

'Why the devil shouldn't we find it? Only got to look up wind. There isn't much of it, but we may have drifted a little further than the pram.'

Pink rigged a light, and *Fiammetta* slowly cast up wind, zigzagging like a busy hound. We came first of all on our wet clothes, which we had thrown down on *Olwen*'s cockpit grating, then on a boat-hook and the cushions, and at last on the pram floating bottom up. Pink fished for her painter, and we hauled her up out of the sea, emptied her and made her fast astern.

The eastern sky now had streaks of grey and the sea was

just visible, like very cold, dark pewter. Pink ran *Fiammetta* to the north, doing a cautious five or six knots. She made water very slowly, and it was plain enough that we could bring her in if we wished. I must admit that, when I thought of the four of us in Pink's eight-foot pram, I was all for doing a hearty spell at the pump and sticking to *Fiammetta* as long as possible. Pink wouldn't have it. He pointed out that visibility was now a good half mile, and that at any moment we might be seen. When I wanted to argue he had to give me a real naval order.

We raided Ritter's wardrobe for clean clothes, and wrapped the children in blankets and brought them on deck. They were breathing quite naturally, and I didn't think it would be long before they woke up. Then we dealt with *Fiammetta*. Her bows were badly crumpled, but the main damage was above the water line. Down in the forepeak were eighteen inches of water. We hadn't an axe, so I cut a splintered, straining plank with what was left in the magazine of Pink's pistol. His iron bar did the rest. After that we had to get out of the forepeak pretty fast.

I lowered the children overboard to Pink – for I could hardly trust myself to stand up in that wretched cockleshell, let alone handle cargo – and we waited at a safe distance to see the last of *Fiammetta*. In five minutes she dipped the great rent in her bows under water, and in another two she was gone.

'Where are we?' I asked Pink.

'If you take that little toy compass of yours and sit quietly in the stern and keep me rowing due north,' he said, 'we're going to land on Weymouth sands in a couple of hours. Oh, muvver, look at them kids what's been out fishing! It don't seem 'ardly safe in that little boat, do it?'

It certainly didn't. We can't have had more than three inches of freeboard. Our fragile solitude was even grimmer in the cold hour of daybreak when the easterly breeze got up, and one could see the ranks of the waves – petty channel waves, but all higher than my shoulders – dancing between white Arish Mell and Portland. They flicked the pram and splashed into my children's faces and woke them up.

Jerry's eyes opened to the sky above him, and took notice of Pink, swinging and smiling. Then he twisted himself round and looked straight into my face.

'Daddy!' he yelled, and tried to jump up. 'George, here's Daddy!'

We shipped a bucketful of water, and I held them fast between my knees.

'Where were you? Who were those men? Where are we? Where's mummy?' – the questions fell over each other.

'Darlings, it was all a mess,' I said. 'We were all going out on a yacht, and then we got separated, and those dam' fools kept you until they could find me. And I was away on a job, and took some finding. It was all rather like the war, you see.'

That phrase explained nothing to them, but meant a lot. They were too young to remember anything of the war. Yet the conversations they had overheard and the endless, curious chattering between themselves and school-fellows had given them a steadfast impression of a world full of separation and anxiety, especially of separation, which, nevertheless, was part of the family tradition and therefore not to be feared – a world inexplicable but enviably exciting, and ennobled, at any rate to children, by the simply understood virtues of duty and courage.

'Were there bombs?' George asked.

'Daddy doesn't mean that kind of war,' Jerry explained with superiority of two extra years. 'Daddy means that he's had to go where he was told.'

'I don't like war,' said George positively. 'I've got a headache.'

I begged them to tell me if they were hurt or hungry. No, they had had a custard trifle for supper, and lots of sardines.

'More sardines than Mummy ever lets us eat,' George added.

Children are queer creatures. They accept pleasure so wholeheartedly in spite of anxiety. Well, may the Lord take Fallot's catering into consideration when he comes up for judgment!

'Nothing like a spot of bailing for keeping warm,' Pink interrupted. 'Now, if one of you two chaps takes the dipper and chucks the water overboard as fast as it comes in, we'll get along fine.'

'*I* will,' said Jerry.

'No, *I* want it,' said George, and rocked the boat.

This was like old times again. I had to lay it down that each would bail for five minutes. They were not at all afraid of the sea. A grown-up awaking in the bottom of that pram would have yelled with alarm. But since Pink and I seemed to accept our position as perfectly normal, so did the children. And what was mere water, I suppose, compared to the overwhelming, long-expected appearance of a parent?

They were exasperatingly calm about their experiences. All I could gather was they had slept a lot, and that the friends whom I had sent to fetch them in my car had been kind, had even played with them when they weren't busy.

'Was it silly of me to be frightened?' George asked, snuggling in between my knees while his brother bailed.

I can find no kinder epitaph for the dead. They deserve that much, and no more.

Pink's reckoning was right. At full dawn we could see the houses of Weymouth, and when the sun rose clear of the Channel clouds we were a mile from the beach. The harsh hiss of the pram's bows on sand was as welcome a sound as ever I heard in my life. We ran her up above high-water mark, and handed her over to the care of a man who hired out motor-boats. I don't know whether he had dealt so long with the public that nothing surprised him, or whether his own seamanship was limited to a holiday beach. He merely said that he would have preferred something bigger himself.

I telephoned Cecily. It was thirty-six hours since she heard of me. The dead, monotonous, *yes?* with which she answered the telephone made my voice break with pity for her. I told her that I had got them, that I was taking a taxi and should be home in three-quarters of an hour. She did not reply for several seconds, but I had no need to ask if she was still there. Then came the flood of maternal questions in the warm, the eager, the beloved voice, and I found myself answering, just as if we had been caught in the rain on an early morning walk, that there was nothing which a hot bath and a good breakfast wouldn't cure.

Pink and his ticks went straight up to London by the morning train. I sent a long wire to Roland, and that was all. I had had enough of Roland's affairs, and I wanted Pink to tell his own story. He met, I gather, with a good deal of scepticism, and they confined him to a room in a cheap hotel during the incubation period while they fed his ticks on an unfortunate bullock. In the same week Holberg disappeared from Tangier, leaving nothing behind him but the wind blowing through his house.

After that, when the bullock and its stall and all but the skin of the attendant vets had been burned, of course I had to go to London and be interviewed by one official after another, all solemn with secrecy. My impression, for what it's worth, was that they were far more terrified of a question being asked in the House than of familiar problems of biological warfare, and that they felt I had shown a lamentable want of tact in not accompanying *Fiammetta* to the bottom of the Channel. But for Pink, who was dealing with less conventional offices of state, nothing was too good; and he came into his own with very little help from me. He is now too thoroughly occupied ever to bother again with visionary politics. If he can manage to stay alive, I feel that he may yet retire to the boatyard he wanted, and run the local Boys' Club and become a Justice of the Peace.

As for me, I shall never forget the joy of that first day at home, and how the wings of our mutual love folded over us and held us. After that, things didn't go so well. I wouldn't speak of what had happened and Cecily was worried about me and I resented it. So, though all that matters has been told, there is, perhaps, one more question to be answered. And indeed I myself, when I have watched the revival of some tragedy, have often wondered how the last man left upon the stage could bear his life thereafter.

It was the children themselves who brought on the crisis. One day, when I was too silent to be teased, they teased their mother, chanting to her *Ruthless Rhymes* which she detests and they dearly love, seeing in them no more relation to life than has a fairy story.

'Oh, mother dear, what is that mess,' they yelled, dancing round her, inspired and soulless imps, 'which looks like strawberry jam?'

I screamed at them in a furious temper, and went out over the downs, ill and ashamed, and didn't come back for hours.

Well, I suppose the dramatist merely assumed that the last man upon the stage went to his priest, and that was that. We, less simple and fortunate, have to put up with more secular authority. But, in fact, a man who has such a wife as I has little need of a psychologist. She saw what was wrong and persuaded me to tell it, and these pages are for her.

More about Penguins

Penguinews, which appears every month, contains details of all the new books issued by Penguins as they are published. From time to time it is supplemented by *Penguins in Print*, which is a complete list of all books published by Penguins which are in print. (There are well over three thousand of these.)

A specimen copy of *Penguinews* will be sent to you free on request, and you can become a subscriber for the price of the postage. For a year's issues (including the complete lists) please send 30p if you live in the United Kingdom, or 60p if you live elsewhere. Just write to Dept EP, Penguin Books Ltd, Harmondsworth, Middlesex, enclosing a cheque or postal order, and your name will be added to the mailing list.

Some other Penguin crime and mystery is described on the following pages.

Note : *Penguinews* and *Penguins in Print* are not available in the U.S.A. or Canada

Murder Makes the Wheels Go Round

Emma Lathen

When three of Michigan Motor's top executives came out of prison, things started happening.

Like murder.

The men had served six months for price fixing. They came out wanting their jobs back and the name of the person who had tipped the authorities about their illegal profit-making deals. They seemed to be getting their own way. Then one of them gets killed. And a fascinating murder hunt starts . . .

Not for sale in the U.S.A. or Canada

Police Blotter

Robert L. Pike

This is just a few days in the life of the 52nd Precinct police station.

It's the story of New York's tidal wave of crime and of a few policemen who feel as effective as Canute in holding it back.

Lieutenant Clancy's blotter carries the ink stains of crimes big and small. From a threatened assassination of a U.N. delegate, to the theft of $16 from a shoe-shine man.

In just a few short days, crime follows crime. Suicide in a crowd. Murder in solitude. Robbery with violence. Violence without reason.

But for Lieutenant Clancy solving these crimes brings no relief. Tomorrow, there'll be new crimes. There is no relief.

Also available

Bullitt

(originally published as *Mute Witness*)